Pizza Cake

Ten funny stories from a
favourite Australian author.

Also by Morris Gleitzman

The Other Facts of Life
Second Childhood
Two Weeks with the Queen
Misery Guts
Worry Warts
Puppy Fat
Blabber Mouth
Sticky Beak
Gift of the Gab
Belly Flop
Water Wings
Wicked! (with Paul Jennings)
Deadly! (with Paul Jennings)
Bumface
Adults Only
Teacher's Pet
Toad Rage
Toad Heaven
Toad Away
Toad Surprise
Boy Overboard
Girl Underground
Worm Story
Aristotle's Nostril
Doubting Thomas
Give Peas a Chance
Grace
Once
Then
Now
Too Small to Fail

Morris Gleitzman

Pizza Cake

AND OTHER FUNNY STORIES

PUFFIN

PUFFIN BOOKS

Published by the Penguin Group
Penguin Books Ltd, 80 Strand, London WC2R 0RL, England
Penguin Group (USA) Inc., 375 Hudson Street, New York, New York 10014, USA
Penguin Group (Canada), 90 Eglinton Avenue East, Suite 700, Toronto, Ontario, Canada M4P 2Y3
(a division of Pearson Penguin Canada Inc.)
Penguin Ireland, 25 St Stephen's Green, Dublin 2, Ireland (a division of Penguin Books Ltd)
Penguin Group (Australia), 250 Camberwell Road, Camberwell, Victoria 3124, Australia
(a division of Pearson Australia Group Pty Ltd)
Penguin Books India Pvt Ltd, 11 Community Centre, Panchsheel Park, New Delhi – 110 017, India
Penguin Group (NZ), 67 Apollo Drive, Rosedale, Auckland 0632, New Zealand
(a division of Pearson New Zealand Ltd)
Penguin Books (South Africa) (Pty) Ltd, Block D, Rosebank Office Park, 181 Jan Smuts Avenue,
Parktown North, Gauteng 2193, South Africa

Penguin Books Ltd, Registered Offices: 80 Strand, London WC2R 0RL, England

puffinbooks.com

Published by Penguin Group (Australia) 2011
Published in Great Britain in Puffin Books 2012
001 – 10 9 8 7 6 5 4 3 2 1

Text copyright © Creative Input Pty Ltd, 2011
Illustrations copyright © Andrew Weldon, 2011
Designed by Tony Palmer, Penguin Group (Australia)
All rights reserved

Slightly different versions of 'Secret Diary of a Dad', 'Draclia', 'Tickled Onions' and 'Big Mistake'
were first published in the Get Reading! collection *Tickled Onions*.

The moral right of the author and illustrator has been asserted

Set in 13/15pt Minion by Post Pre-press Group, Brisbane, Queensland
Printed in Great Britain by Clays Ltd, St Ives plc

British Library Cataloguing in Publication Data
A CIP catalogue record for this book is available from the British Library

ISBN: 978-0-141-34371-6

www.greenpenguin.co.uk

For my sister Melanie

Contents

Saving Ms Fosdyke   1

Pizza Cake   15

Charles The Second   37

Secret Diary Of A Dad   53

Can't Complain   71

Draclia   85

Tickled Onions   101

Stationery Is Never Stationary   121

Big Mistake   137

Harriet's Story   149

Saving Ms Fosdyke

Dad was flabbergasted when I told him the news.

He nearly dropped the plate he was washing up. He stared at me, water dripping off his elbows.

'Fifty million?' he said. 'Your school is selling Ms Fosdyke to West Chirnside Primary for fifty million pounds?'

I nodded sadly.

'That's crazy,' said Dad. 'They could get heaps more for a teacher like her. The primary school near the library just paid over seventy million for a year-four teacher with half her experience.'

Mum nodded as she took the plate from him and dried it.

'And that was a bargain,' she said. 'Last week the high school paid a hundred million pounds for a maths teacher.'

'Crazy,' said Dad. 'Giving away a top teacher like

1

Ms Fosdyke for fifty million. You don't even get a good footballer for that these days.'

I agreed. It was crazy.

And it was all my fault.

'Emmy, love, don't chew your pen,' said Mum. 'Those pens cost nearly a pound each. Have you finished your homework?'

'Almost,' I said. 'I'm doing my creative writing task. I'm making up a story about some teachers who are badly paid and overworked and don't get much respect.'

Mum frowned.

'Sounds a bit far-fetched,' she said.

'It's a fantasy story,' I said. 'Ms Fosdyke encourages us to use our imagination.'

Dad wiped his hands and picked up my exercise book and read a couple of sentences. He frowned and put the exercise book down again.

'Even fantasy stories need to be a little bit believable, Emmy,' he said. 'You can't just write totally impossible crazy stuff.'

Mum sat down next to me at the kitchen table and put her arm round me.

'You must be feeling sad,' she said. 'About Ms Fosdyke being transferred.'

I nodded.

Mum and Dad both looked sympathetic.

Suddenly I knew I had to risk it and tell them. So they'd see why it was so important that Ms Fosdyke didn't leave.

'Ms Fosdyke thinks that one day . . .'

I hesitated for a sec. Was this going to sound dopey?

'. . . that one day I could be a teacher.'

Mum and Dad just stared at me. They were both flabbergasted.

'A teacher?' said Mum.

'Are you sure?' said Dad.

I nodded.

'Oh love,' said Mum. 'That might be pushing it a bit. Why don't you lower your sights just a little. What about being a doctor? Or a lawyer?'

'I want to be a teacher,' I said quietly. 'I want to help people's minds blossom like Ms Fosdyke does.'

Mum sighed.

'Emmy,' she said. 'Only the smartest, cleverest, most brilliant people get to be teachers. You know that. It's good to be ambitious, but it's not good to set yourself up for disappointment.'

'Airline pilot,' said Dad. 'Why not give that a try? That's more sensible, eh?'

I didn't reply.

Mum and Dad meant well, but the trouble was they didn't really believe in me. Not really. Not like Ms Fosdyke.

That's why I had to stop her going.

The next day I asked Dad to drop me off early at school.

He said he would, but halfway there the van got

a puncture and by the time he'd fixed it he was late for his first job, which was a leaky toilet, so I had to walk the rest of the way.

When I got to school, the bell had gone. In the playground, the volunteer parents were lining everyone up in class rows.

I ducked down behind the only car in the staff carpark. Ms Fosdyke's Lamborghini. She always came in early to do her marking. That was one of the ways she was different to the other teachers. She reckoned teachers should do their own marking and not just get big law firms to do it.

I crept into school without anyone seeing me.

As I hurried down the corridor, all the staffrooms were quiet. I wasn't surprised. Most of the other teachers didn't come in till ten. Eleven if they felt like a lie-in. But I knew Ms Fosdyke would be in her staffroom.

I tapped on her door.

I could hear voices inside. The radio probably. Ms Fosdyke often listened to the radio while she did her marking so she could find out what was happening in the world and let us kids know. She also went overseas in the school holidays, but you couldn't see everything in only four trips a year, not even when you had your own plane.

The door opened.

'Hello, Emmy,' said Ms Fosdyke, staring at me, surprised, but in a nice way. 'Is everything OK?'

She looked amazing. She was wearing a knitted

silk and cashmere dress with real gold thread at the neck and cuffs, tastefully matched with a Hermes scarf with her own initials on it.

I know about this stuff because Mum works in a drycleaners.

'Everything's not OK, is it Emmy?' said Ms Fosdyke gently.

'Please don't go,' I said. '6F needs you. You're worth more than fifty million pounds to us.'

Ms Fosdyke sighed. Not in an impatient way, in a concerned way.

'Come in,' she said. 'Let's have a talk.'

I followed Ms Fosdyke into her staffroom.

'Have a seat,' she said.

I sat down on a soft white leather sofa, hoping I didn't have any tap grease on the back of my skirt from Dad's van.

'Would you like a juice?' asked Ms Fosdyke. 'I've got apple, cranberry, mango, watermelon, mandarin, peach, pineapple or lychee.'

'No thanks,' I said.

'Doughnut?' she said.

Normally I'd have said yes, specially as Ms Fosdyke had her own Krispy Kreme display case, but I was feeling a bit overwhelmed by actually being in a teacher's own private staffroom.

Except, now I looked around, I saw that Ms Fosdyke's staffroom wasn't quite as huge as I'd thought it would be. She didn't have a jacuzzi or a round bed or a disco floor, not like some teachers.

And her TV wasn't much bigger than ours at home. The paintings on her wall were better, though. She had one that we had, the waterlily one by that French bloke. But hers were done with real paint rather than just printed.

'Emmy,' said Ms Fosdyke, sitting next to me on the lounge. 'It doesn't have to change anything, me leaving. You'll still study hard and go to university, and eventually you'll be a really good teacher, I know you will.'

I mumbled something about how I couldn't do it without her.

'You can,' said Ms Fosdyke. 'I used to be just like you. I used to look at teachers and think, how could I ever do that job, the most important and prestigious and highest-paid and hard-to-get job in the world?'

'Exactly,' I said.

'Get real, my dad used to say,' sighed Ms Fosdyke. 'Be a brain surgeon.'

'Really?' I said.

Ms Fosdyke nodded.

'But I wanted to teach,' she said. 'So I made myself have courage.'

Before I could ask her how, the toilet in her ensuite bathroom flushed and a man came out. He was much older than Ms Fosdyke and wearing a business suit. I wondered if he was an uncle of hers. One who'd encouraged her to be teacher. And to say thank you, she let him use her private bathroom.

'Emmy,' said Ms Fosdyke, 'this is Joe Greely, my agent.'

I knew what an agent was. A sort of business manager. You have to have one when you earn as much as a teacher does.

'That name rings an unpleasant bell,' said Mr Greely, frowning at me. 'Emily. It was you who put this whole West Chirnside idea into Debra's head, right?'

'It's Emmy,' I said in a small voice.

But he was right, it was me who told Ms Fosdyke about West Chirnside Primary and how they didn't have enough teachers because they couldn't afford them, and how my cousin's year-three class was being taught by the school caretaker.

Now I wished I hadn't. I should have guessed that a kind and wonderful teacher like Ms Fosdyke wouldn't be able to control herself when she heard about a school where a whole year-three class was only learning about door-hinge oil and leaf-blowing. And that she'd offer herself to the poor school, even though they couldn't really afford her.

It was all my fault. If I'd kept quiet, Ms Fosdyke wouldn't be leaving us.

'Don't blame Emmy for this, Joe,' said Ms Fosdyke. 'It's my decision.'

Mr Greely helped himself to a drink that didn't look like juice from Ms Fosdyke's cocktail bar, and a doughnut. He kept giving me looks and I could tell he did blame me.

I decided that if I was ever a teacher I'd insist on having a much lower wage than normal so I wouldn't need an agent.

Except I knew I probably wouldn't ever be a teacher, so it didn't matter.

'Fifty million,' said Mr Greely to Ms Fosdyke with a scowl. 'Creyton College would have coughed up a hundred and twenty million for you, even though you're stubborn and pig-headed.'

'We've been through this,' said Ms Fosdyke, sounding almost as annoyed as she did when she lent the year-six science club her very own electron microscope and they dropped it. 'I'm a teacher. I'm not doing this job for the money. I go where children need me.'

I was about to point out to Ms Fosdyke that the children at our school needed her too, but Mr Greely butted in.

'West Chirnside haven't even got the full fifty,' he said.

'I don't care,' said Ms Fosdyke. 'Do you know how many cake stalls and fetes a school fundraising committee has to put on to raise fifty million pounds?'

She paused.

'How much have they got?' she asked.

'Forty-seven million, six hundred and thirty-two thousand, nine hundred and twenty-eight pounds,' said Mr Greely grumpily. 'So that's even less of a fee I get.'

'You do OK,' said Ms Fosdyke. 'Anyway, some

things are more important than a measly two and a half million. Right now I'd rather you were concerned about a little girl who's feeling very sad.'

Ms Fosdyke turned back to me, and for a few moments her shoulders slumped.

Then she gave my arm a gentle squeeze, stood up, and tossed her head so her fantastic haircut flopped perfectly into place.

I know about this stuff because my auntie works in a dog-trimming parlour.

'I'm sorry, Emmy,' said Ms Fosdyke. 'I've loved being at this school, but I've given West Chirnside my word.'

She sighed and poured herself a juice.

Suddenly I realised what was happening.

Ms Fosdyke was feeling sad too. And trapped. She'd made West Chirnside Primary a promise, but now she was about to leave us, she didn't want to go. And was wishing somebody could get her out of it.

I stood up.

'Thanks for the talk, Ms Fosdyke,' I said. 'I should be off to class now.'

I needed to get there as quickly as possible.

To start planning how to save Ms Fosdyke.

Ms Fosdyke was a bit late getting to class.

The volunteer warm-up parent was starting to look anxious. He'd done all his warm-up things twice, and was just starting us on our times tables for the third time when Ms Fosdyke arrived.

'Sorry,' said Ms Fosdyke after the applause and cheering had died down. 'It's turning into a bit of a morning.'

I didn't mind, because the extra time had given me a chance to work out exactly what we were going to do to save Ms Fosdyke.

My plan was to wait until the volunteer warm-up parent left, then get all the biggest kids in the class to lie down against the door and barricade it shut. Then I'd ring the TV news and tell them we were holding Ms Fosdyke hostage, but in a good way. And when they asked what our demands were, I'd tell them we only had one. That West Chirnside Primary School spend their forty-seven and a bit million pounds on a different teacher.

The volunteer warm-up parent said goodbye and left.

Which was a bit sudden. I wasn't ready. I didn't have the phone number for the TV news, and I hadn't explained my plan to the rest of the class.

I waited till Ms Fosdyke started the lesson, which was a group conversation about personal choices in life. Then I got my phone out and googled under the desk and found the TV news number.

I sent a text to all the other kids explaining my plan. Trouble was, they were all enjoying being part of the conversation so much, they didn't notice.

I decided I'd have to start the plan on my own and explain it as I went along. I knew I wasn't big enough to barricade the door without help, but once I was lying there, the others would get the idea and join in.

I stood up.

And saw something weird through the class-room window.

A TV news cameraman was outside in the corridor with some other TV news people. Which was amazing because I hadn't even rung them yet.

Ms Fosdyke saw me standing up. Then she saw the TV news people in the corridor. Mr Greely was with them.

'I'm sorry,' Ms Fosdyke said to us. 'Looks like we're going to have a bit of an interruption. I'm guessing it's my agent's idea. He's probably thinking that if I'm going to a poor underprivileged school, I might as well get some publicity for it.'

She gave Mr Greely a glare, and I could see she wasn't happy.

I wasn't either. Once this was on the news, and the nation was saying what a saint Ms Fosdyke was, she'd have to keep her word to West Chirnside. I wondered if I should fling myself against the door and try to keep the TV news crew out.

Before I could, they came in.

One of them introduced himself as the director and asked me to sit down and told the class not to wave at the camera.

Another one, who you could tell was a reporter because she was reporting, explained to the camera what an unusual teacher Ms Fosdyke was. Then she interviewed Mr Greely, who agreed that Ms Fosdyke was a very unusual teacher, and said that her generosity was priceless. He also said that after Ms Fosdyke finished her two-year contract with West Chirnside, she'd be available for transfer to another school for a hundred and fifty million pounds.

The director asked Ms Fosdyke if they could film some scenes in the classroom that would show viewers what an unusual teacher she was.

'Sure,' said Ms Fosdyke. 'I'm feeling a bit tired, so I'm going to ask Emmy to take the class for a while.'

I was sitting down, but I almost fell over.

'Me?' I croaked.

Ms Fosdyke smiled and beckoned me out the front.

Everybody was looking at me.

I went and stood in front of the class. The TV news people switched on a couple more lights and out of the corner of my eye I could see the camera staring at me.

The class was staring at me too, stunned.

'What do you want me to do?' I whispered to Ms Fosdyke.

'Up to you,' she said. 'You're the teacher.'

I was on the news that night.

They didn't show all my lesson, because it went for nearly twenty minutes and that wouldn't have left time for several wars and a new polar bear cub at the zoo.

But they had nearly thirty seconds of it, enough to show how brilliant 6F were at getting over their camera nerves and coming up with some great ideas in the thought experiment I did with them.

We were brainstorming about teachers, and what the world would be like if they were overworked and underpaid and didn't get much respect.

Garth Webster, who was usually one of the shyest in the class, said a really good thing about how teachers wouldn't be able to give the best of themselves if they had to worry about their car repair bills and their blood pressure and their social lives. I reckon Garth might be a TV host one day.

After the segment finished, I glanced at Mum and Dad.

They were both staring at me, mouths open.

'You were amazing,' said Mum.

'Blimey,' said Dad. 'I think we're going to be better off in our old age than we thought.'

I knew that was just his way of letting me know how proud he was.

'Don't choose a mansion yet,' I said. 'If I do get to be a teacher, I'm probably going to be working in a fairly poor school.'

Mum and Dad didn't look like they were too upset by that.

Not as upset as they were by the sudden thought Mum had.

'We should have recorded that segment,' Mum wailed.

I didn't mind we hadn't, because I knew I'd never forget it.

Specially the last shot of Ms Fosdyke smiling, her kind eyes shining and her expertly-whitened teeth gleaming. I know about that stuff because Dad's best friend is a tiler.

On the screen you couldn't see who she was smiling at.

She was smiling at me.

Thanks, Ms Fosdyke.

Whatever they pay you in the future, you're worth every penny.

Pizza Cake

The changing room looks like a battlefield.

Not one of those battlefields you see in old war photos.

A cricket battlefield.

Glenn can hardly bear to look. He forces himself to. This is his team and they're in pain. Most of them are either slumped on the benches groaning, or lying on the floor thinking about groaning.

It'll be his turn in about ten minutes.

'That bowler should be banned,' mutters Daisy Taylor, one of the openers. She's holding a damp bunched-up towel to her forehead.

'There should be a law against people in year six bowling that fast,' says Stefano Priori, batsman number three, hugging his bruised arm. 'Bowling that fast isn't natural. I reckon that kid's mum gives him steroids. And I bet he's got one of those exercise machines from daytime TV.'

The rest of the Dudley Park Primary School team murmur their agreement from the floor.

Outside on the oval there's another explosion of cheering. Glenn sighs. More delight from the St Catherine's Primary School parents and players. Another wicket down. And probably another Dudley Park batsman down too.

Only numbers eight, nine and ten to go, thinks Glenn nervously. And then it's my turn.

'Come on, Dougal,' he says. 'You're number eight.'

Dougal McCoy stands up, his pads only half-buckled, flaps across the changing room and locks himself in the toilet.

'Dougal,' groans Glenn. 'You can't do that now.'

Mr Leung comes in with his arm round Desiree Walsh's shoulders. Desiree, number seven, is limping. And crying.

'She'll be OK,' says Mr Leung. 'She fell on her wicket.'

'I was pushed,' sobs Desiree. 'By the ball.'

Glenn gives Desiree a sympathetic look and a damp bunched-up towel.

Easy for teachers to talk about being OK, thinks Glenn. Teachers don't have cricket balls hurtling towards them at four hundred kilometres an hour.

'Mr Leung,' he says out loud. 'I think we should declare.'

Mr Leung stares at Glenn, speechless for a second. But only a second.

'Dudley Primary does not declare,' says Mr

Leung. 'Specially not at six for thirteen.'

Glenn wants to remind Mr Leung that cricket is meant to be fun rather than life-threatening. But Mr Leung is already asking who's batting next.

There's a silence.

Dougal's plaintive voice comes from behind the toilet door.

'I've got the squirts.'

Mr Leung frowns.

'Somebody has to go in next,' he says.

He looks around the changing room. So does Glenn.

Ralph Watson (number nine) is hiding behind the swimming floaties. Mia Katsiannis (number ten) is pretending she's already batted and has been knocked unconscious.

'I'll bat next,' says Glenn.

He starts buckling his pads on.

If somebody has to go in, he thinks grimly, it might as well be me. At least I've got something the others haven't.

Mr Leung gives him a not-very-encouraging look. Glenn knows what Mr Leung is thinking. Glenn Gershwin, number eleven, worst batsman in the team. Won't even last one ball.

'Go on then,' says Mr Leung. 'Get it over with.'

As Glenn leaves the changing room, he sees the team are all watching him. A couple (numbers nine and ten) are giving him grateful looks. Most of the others are staring at him as if he's mad.

'Just try and get your bat behind the ball,' says Mr Leung.

Thank you Mr Leung, thinks Glenn as he heads towards the smirking St Catherine's parents and players. I wouldn't have thought of that.

Glenn takes his time walking to the middle of the oval, partly to give his hands a chance to stop shaking and partly so he can finish chewing.

He reaches the wicket, swallows, takes guard with his bat, and squints down the pitch at the bowler.

Who is big.

Very big.

Stefano's right, thinks Glenn. That kid's mum is giving him something. Steroids, vitamins, organic beef, something.

The bowler takes a very long run-up.

Glenn takes a very deep breath.

He tells himself to remember Grandad.

Be brave, he thinks. Don't step back. Don't try to get out of the way of the ball.

The ball hurtles out of the bowler's hand. Sally Pung (number six) turns away at the other end as if she can't bear to look.

Glenn takes a step forward. The ball thunders into the centre of his bat. Shock waves shudder up his arms.

The ball rolls along the pitch back towards the bowler, who looks stunned that Glenn isn't on the ground, bleeding.

Cheers erupt from the Dudley Park parents.

Glenn starts breathing again.

That wasn't so bad.

The next ball is even faster. Glenn takes a bigger step forward. The ball snicks off the edge of the bat. Glenn closes his eyes, waiting for delighted yells from the fielders after he's been caught. But the only delighted yells come from the Dudley parents.

Glenn turns and sees the ball rolling over the boundary line.

Four runs.

The bowler is glaring so hard his eyebrows look like they're joined. He turns and walks back for an even longer run-up.

Glenn smiles to himself. Thanks to Grandad, this isn't so hard after all.

'Pizza cake,' he whispers to himself.

After the match, as Glenn is walking home, Dougal catches him up.

'You were amazing,' says Dougal. 'Seventeen not out. Top scorer. Amazing.'

Dougal is bouncing with excitement, despite the lump on his forehead.

Glenn glances at Dougal's shining eyes, concerned. He hopes it's just enthusiasm rather than concussion.

'You were amazing too,' says Glenn. 'Mine were mostly lucky runs. Your four runs were great.'

'They weren't really runs,' says Dougal. 'They're called leg byes when the ball bounces off your head and goes to the boundary.'

'They're still runs,' says Glenn. 'We wouldn't have won without them.'

'We wouldn't have won without your amazing fielding,' says Dougal. 'Nine catches. How brave were you, fielding so close to their batsmen.'

'It's called silly point,' says Glenn, starting to feel a bit embarrassed by Dougal's praise.

'I'd call it fearless point,' says Dougal. 'You totally messed with their minds, standing less than a metre away from them.'

Glenn doesn't say anything.

He wants to change the subject before Dougal starts asking how he manages to be so brave. But before he can, Dougal's face drops.

'I wish I was as brave as you,' says Dougal.

'You were very brave,' says Glenn. 'After you dropped those four catches, you didn't cry or go home or anything. You stayed on the pitch and stopped the ball several times with your body.'

'I was trying to duck,' mutters Dougal, rubbing his ribs. 'I wasn't as brave as you.'

'Hey, it's the weekend tomorrow,' says Glenn, changing the subject. 'Doing anything good?'

Dougal looks even gloomier.

'Tomorrow morning,' he says, 'I've got to do the scariest thing in my life.'

Glenn looks at him.

He wonders what the scariest thing in Dougal's life could be. Going round to the big bowler's place and demanding money for medical treatment?

Probably not.

'My nan died on Tuesday,' says Dougal. 'Her funeral's tomorrow morning. I've got to stand up in front of everybody in a big church and talk about her.'

'That's tough,' says Glenn. 'It's hard to get words out when you're feeling really sad.'

'It's not the sad words that's worrying me,' says Dougal. 'It's the huge crowd I have to say them to.'

Glenn nods. He understands about public speaking. He had to introduce a visiting author on stage once in front of the whole school, and it was the scariest experience of his life.

Or it would have been without his secret weapon.

'I loved Nan and I want to do a good job,' Dougal is saying. 'But hundreds of people will be looking at me and I'll probably panic and I won't be able to speak and if they start laughing I might try to run outside but I'll probably pick the wrong door and get wedged behind the christening font and they'll have to get the fire brigade to rescue me and I'll be on the national news and everyone at school will be laughing too.'

Dougal stops and holds onto a fence for a moment. Glenn isn't sure if Dougal is out of breath or dizzy with fear. Probably both.

Poor bloke.

For a moment Glenn is tempted to tell Dougal his secret. The secret of being brave. But what if Dougal thinks it's stupid? What if he laughs or scoffs? And what if, after that, the secret doesn't work any more?

What then?

'I'll never be as brave as you,' says Dougal sadly. 'When you were fielding at fearless point, you weren't wearing extra padding or anything. You were completely unprotected.'

'Not completely,' says Glenn. 'I did have some protection.'

What am I doing? he thinks. I'm telling Dougal my secret.

'The plastic thing over your goolies?' says Dougal. 'That doesn't count. Everyone has that. I had two on when I was batting.'

Glenn shakes his head.

'My protection was in my back pocket,' he says.

Dougal stares at him for a moment, puzzled.

'Bandaids?' says Dougal.

Glenn shakes his head again.

Tell him, he says to himself. Dougal's your friend. He needs your help.

'Pizza,' says Glenn.

Dougal stares at the old photo of Grandad, amazed.

'Your grandfather climbed into that castle with his bare hands?' he says. 'While Nazis were shooting at him? And when he got inside he took them all prisoner? On his own?'

Glenn nods.

'Amazing,' says Dougal.

'Keep your voice down,' whispers Glenn. 'For some reason Mum doesn't like me looking at Grandad's photo album.'

He glances at his bedroom door. It's tightly shut, so with a bit of luck no noise is leaking out.

Dougal turns the page in the album.

'Wow,' he whispers. 'Is that a Nazi tank?'

Glenn nods again.

'Grandad invented a way of capturing tanks by jumping onto them from trees,' he says. 'It was so successful, all the resistance fighters in Czechoslovakia started using it.'

Dougal's eyes are shining as he stares at the faded photo.

'Your grandad was a war hero,' he says.

'Yes,' says Glenn quietly. 'He was.'

'No wonder you're so brave,' says Dougal. 'When you were little, he probably gave you bravery lessons.'

'Sort of,' says Glenn.

Dougal turns to the next page and stares again.

'Is that your grandad up that mountain?' he says.

'When he first came to Australia after the war,' says Glenn, 'he went to work on a big dam in the Snowy Mountains. But because he was so brave, he spent a fair bit of time rescuing mountain climbers.'

'That looks like a goat he's carrying on his back,' says Dougal.

'And goats,' says Glenn.

Dougal turns the page. His eyes go even wider. Glen sees that Dougal has found the photo of Grandad swimming through rough seas towards a damaged passenger boat with a rope in his mouth.

'He was a volunteer in the State Emergency Service all his life,' says Glenn. 'Well, not quite all his life. They made him resign when he was seventy-six.'

'I wish I had somebody that brave in my family,' says Dougal wistfully. He frowns. 'Except I don't understand, what's all this got to do with pizza?'

'When Grandad was very old,' says Glenn, 'me and him used to look at his photos together. I used to ask him how he did all these incredibly brave things. He used to just shrug and say pizza cake.'

'Huh?' says Dougal.

'I couldn't ever get him to explain exactly what he meant,' says Glenn. 'But after he died, I worked it out.'

'Pizza cake?' says Dougal.

'Pizza cake,' says Glenn.

'What's pizza cake?' says Dougal.

'Glenn, my man,' says Rick.

Glenn waits as usual while Rick wipes the flour off his hands, glances at the pizza oven to make sure nothing's burning, and gives him a high-five.

'You're early,' says Rick.

Then he sees Dougal and hesitates.

'It's OK,' says Glenn. 'Dougal's in on the secret.'

Rick looks surprised, then shrugs.

'Your call,' he says. 'You know my motto. What happens in the pizza shop stays in the pizza shop. I'm a pizza guy, not a social worker. Or a dentist. Your friends and your teeth are your business.'

While he's talking he grabs several lumps of pizza dough, twirls them till they're flat, and lays them out on the pizza board.

'What do you fancy?' he says.

'Same as last week, please,' says Glenn. 'Marshmallows, Maltesers, Mars Bars, strawberry jam and peanut butter. And on top, jelly snakes, liquorice bullets, sour sucks, chocolate sultanas, dried pineapple and sugar frosties.'

'You're the boss,' says Rick.

Glenn hands Rick the usual supermarket bag. Rick pulls out the ingredients and starts putting them onto the pizza bases.

'Wow,' breathes Dougal. 'Amazing.'

'It's an art,' says Glenn.

'Not many people realise that,' says Rick.

When the pizza bases are covered, Rick stacks them one on top of the other, adds the jelly snakes, liquorice bullets, sour sucks, chocolate sultanas, dried apricots and sugar frosties, and then the final ingredient.

'Is that cheese?' says Dougal doubtfully.

'Unsalted,' says Rick. 'It's delicious. Trust us.'

He puts the pizza cake into the oven.

'Eight minutes,' he says. 'Have a seat.'

While Glenn and Dougal wait, and Rick serves other customers, Dougal bombards Glenn with questions. Glenn doesn't mind. He was expecting it.

'How can you afford one of those every week?' says Dougal.

'Pocket money,' says Glenn. 'Plus I do weekend jobs for rellies.'

'And you just carry it around with you?' says Dougal. 'Doesn't it go mouldy?'

'Sugar's a preservative,' says Glenn. 'After the pizza cake's cooled, we cut it into slices and wrap them up. I always have a slice with me in case I need it.'

'And,' says Dougal, 'when you want to be brave you just eat some?'

Glenn nods.

'Amazing,' says Dougal. 'How does it actually work, scientifically?'

This is the question Glenn was hoping Dougal wouldn't ask.

'I don't actually know, scientifically,' says Glenn. 'I just know it works. It used to work for Grandad and it works for me.'

'Such as yesterday at cricket,' says Dougal.

'Any time I need to be brave,' says Glenn. 'Like last weekend at a family barbie when I knew aunties would be kissing me after they'd been eating garlic. And the week before that when I had to go up onto the school roof to get my bag. Or when I have to go

26

to the dentist. Or my cousin's school musical. Or change our neighbour's baby's nappy.'

Glenn pauses for breath. Dougal is starting to look more hopeful than Glenn has seen him look for ages.

'Remember when they made me introduce the visiting author in assembly?' says Glenn. 'I had some pizza cake just before I went on stage and I was fine.'

'I remember,' says Dougal. 'We couldn't believe you did it. So it works with public speaking too?'

'Definitely,' says Glenn. 'Have a few bites before you go to your gran's funeral tomorrow morning and you'll be fine.'

Dougal stares at the pizza oven, eyes shining.

'Thank you,' he says to Glenn. 'You've saved my life.'

Glenn opens his eyes.

He blinks a few times. He's in bed and it's morning. He can tell it's morning because Mum is standing in his doorway telling him to get up.

'It's Saturday,' mumbles Glenn.

'I know it's Saturday,' says Mum. 'That's why I want you to tidy your room. So I can vacuum.'

Glenn groans.

Mum starts picking things up off his floor.

Go away, Mum, pleads Glenn silently. I don't need reminding how to tidy a room.

'I'll do it,' he mumbles.

Mum stops picking things up.

But not, Glenn sees, because of what he just said. Because she's staring at something in her hand.

Grandad's photo album.

'Glenn,' sighs Mum. 'You know I don't like you looking at this.'

'I know,' says Glenn. 'Sorry. But they're only photos.'

'They're more than photos,' says Mum. 'They're the silly trophies of a reckless man who caused a lot of worry to the people who loved him.'

Glenn hates it when Mum talks about Grandad like this. He was a brave hero. And her dad.

'All my childhood it was the same,' says Mum. 'He used to come home battered and bruised, one crazy escapade after another. Every time he left the house, we thought we'd never see him again.'

'Didn't you think he was brave?' says Glenn.

'We thought he was selfish,' says Mum. 'We begged him not to go off on any more rescues. But every time all he'd say was, piece of cake.'

Glenn stares at Mum.

She's never said this before.

'You mean pizza cake,' he says.

Mum looks at him, puzzled.

'Pizza cake?' she says. 'No, he used to say piece of cake. It's a stupid expression that means something's as easy as eating a piece of cake. Which, when it involves mountains or storms at sea, it's not.'

Glenn sits up in bed.

Cold panic is starting to churn his insides.

'You didn't hear it properly,' he says to Mum. 'What Grandad used to say was pizza cake.'

Mum gives a bitter laugh.

'I lived with him for about twenty years longer than you did,' she says. 'Trust me, it was piece of cake.'

'No,' says Glenn. 'Pizza cake.'

Mum rolls her eyes. She calls out to Dad, who is shambling towards the bathroom.

'What was it my father used to say each time he went off to try to get killed?'

Dad pauses and hitches up his pyjama trousers.

'Something about taking the biscuit?' he says. 'No, hang on, piece of cake.'

'Thank you,' says Mum.

She turns triumphantly to Glenn.

But Glenn isn't arguing any more. He's flopped back into bed, sick with panic. He's trying not to think about how his life has just fallen apart.

The stupid risks he's taken.

Unprotected.

The rest of his life, scarily ahead of him.

Totally unprotected.

Glenn struggles out of bed. He can't let himself think these thoughts. Not yet.

First he has to get to the church and warn Dougal.

Dougal was right. St Catherine's is a big church.

Very big.

Glenn recognises it as soon as he sprints out

of the side street. It's the church where they had Grandad's funeral.

Glenn crouches on the front steps, gasping for breath after running all the way from home. Once his breathing gets quieter, he creeps closer to the big doors and listens.

He can't hear sounds of laughter. Or jeering. And there's no fire engine out the front. It's not too late. He's in time to warn Dougal.

Glenn opens the door a crack.

The church is full of people. Hundreds. Glenn closes the door.

OK, he says to himself. This is going to be scary, walking in among all those strangers and finding Dougal and getting him out of there before he makes a fool of himself. It's going to be one of the scariest things I've ever done. Specially if Dougal is angry with me for being wrong about pizza cake. What if he loses it and gets violent? And chases me through the wrong door and I get wedged behind the christening font and they have to get the fire brigade to rescue me and I'm on the national news and everyone at school laughs at me for the rest of my life?

Glenn pulls himself together.

Time for a quick couple of mouthfuls.

He reaches into his pocket.

And remembers.

For a second he wants to run. To the nearest bed and hide under the covers. Forever.

But he can't.

He has to warn Dougal.

Glenn pushes open the door and goes in.

Too late. The minister's voice is booming around the huge church, introducing Dougal. A proud grandson who wants to say a few words about his beloved nan. Dougal is standing up. He's walking to the front of the church. He turns and faces the congregation.

Glenn waves frantically at him.

I'm too far up the back, thinks Glenn anxiously. He'll never see me.

But Dougal does.

He squints at Glenn, gives him a little wave, a quick thumbs up and pats the pocket of his funeral trousers. Then he squares his shoulders and starts speaking in a loud and fairly confident voice.

'It's a miracle my nan fits in there,' says Dougal, pointing to the coffin behind him. 'Cause her heart is bigger than . . . than . . .'

Oh no, thinks Glenn, here we go.

'. . . than a cricket oval,' says Dougal.

A gentle wave of fond laughter ripples around the church.

Dougal beams.

Glenn watches anxiously.

'I want to tell you some of the things her big heart did for us all,' says Dougal, sounding more confident with every word.

Of course he's confident, thinks Glenn. He

doesn't know yet. He still thinks the pizza cake is helping him.

Glenn wonders how to break the news.

But he stays silent, partly because he's scared to butt in, and partly because he's slowly realising something.

The pizza cake *is* helping Dougal. It's helping him because he believes it will.

Just because I can't ever be brave again, thinks Glenn, that's no reason Dougal can't. He can get his own pizza cake each week and have a fearless life. As long as I don't tell him.

Glenn slips quietly out of the church.

He reaches the street, and heads towards his place. Then he stops. He turns round and walks in the opposite direction towards the cemetery.

It's months since he's visited Grandad's grave.

This feels like a good time to do it.

The cemetery is quite big, and Glenn gets a bit lost for a while, but he finds the grave at last.

'Hello, Grandad,' he says, standing in front of the marble slab. 'You probably think I'm a bit of a dope. But thanks anyway. The pizza cake helped me a lot, even though you probably haven't got a clue what it is.'

To fill Grandad in, Glenn lists the times pizza cake helped him be brave. The garlic aunties and the school roof and the pooey nappies, everything.

By the time Glenn has finished, he's starving.

He remembers why. He sprinted out of the house without any breakfast, and now he's weak with hunger.

He goes through his pockets. Nothing. Just a piece of pizza cake left over from yesterday.

Glenn sits on the end of Grandad's grave and eats it. Now that it's just cake, it's actually a bit too sweet. But when you haven't had breakfast it's better than nothing.

While he chews, Glenn has a thought.

All those brave things Grandad did, he did them on his own.

Without pizza cake.

How?

Glenn stares at the shiny black marble of Grandad's headstone.

Maybe, he thinks, when you've done something a few times, it gets a bit easier. Grandad spent his whole life being brave, which gave him plenty of experience at it.

Glenn realises he can see his own reflection in the headstone.

Me too, he thinks. I've had a fair bit of experience of being brave too.

'Look who it isn't,' says a loud sneering voice.

Startled, Glenn looks up. Looming over him is a tough-looking boy he vaguely recognises.

Oh no.

It's the big bowler from yesterday.

Glenn stands up.

'What are you doing here?' says the boy with a threatening scowl. 'This is our cemetery.'

'How can it be your cemetery?' says Glenn.

'My dead uncle's buried here,' says the boy. 'He died in a karate accident. But not before he taught me everything he knew.'

The boy takes a couple of steps closer to Glenn. Now he's standing very close.

Suddenly Glenn understands. The church down the street. And the school next to it. St Catherine's.

'You're dead meat,' says the boy. 'You might have fluked a win against us at cricket, but it was a big mistake coming over here for a gloat.'

Glenn struggles to keep his voice from wobbling.

'I'm not gloating,' he says. 'I'm visiting my dead grandad. He died in a hang-gliding accident. But not before he taught me everything he knew.'

The boy hesitates. Then he scowls again.

'Smarty pants, eh?' he says. 'This the old codger's grave here, is it? Good, I need a leak and all this marble looks exactly like a bathroom to me.'

He starts to unzip his fly.

Glenn takes a step forward and stares directly up into the boy's eyes.

'Remember yesterday,' he says, 'when I wasn't scared of your bowling? That's because I'm fearless. You've probably never tangled with a fearless person before, have you?'

Feeling sick, he waits for this to sink in, his eyes not leaving the boy's.

After what seems to Glenn like several years, the boy looks away. And zips his pants back up.

'Not wasting good pee here,' growls the boy. 'We've got a lemon tree at home needs it.'

He stamps away.

Suddenly Glenn's legs don't feel completely fearless any more. He sits back down on the corner of Grandad's grave and takes a few moments to recover. He catches sight of his own reflection again in the shiny marble.

There's a grin on his face.

He's never felt like this before.

Trembling, but really good.

He gives Grandad a thumbs up.

Then, once his legs start working again, Glenn heads back towards the church to meet Dougal after the service.

On the way he thinks about the big bowler and hears himself say something he's never said before. He says it very quietly. So quietly he's not completely sure it's him saying it, but he's pretty sure it is.

'Piece of cake.'

Charles The Second

My name is Charles Rennie Mackintosh and I wish it wasn't.

I'm nervy enough as it is. The last thing I need is a name everyone thinks is hilarious.

Well, not everyone. Mostly just the kids in my class.

'Look, it's Charles Rennie Mackintosh,' they say several times a day. 'Could that be the legendary early-twentieth-century Scottish furniture design genius?'

Everyone sniggers because they know what's coming next.

'Oh no,' they say. 'Our mistake. It's just farty-pants.'

They're right, I'm not the legendary early-twentieth-century Scottish furniture design genius. I was born in Australia but now we live in London. I'm in year seven. I don't even do woodwork.

And I am a bit of a farty-pants.

I've tried every type of diet to stop it. Meat-free, wheat-free, dairy-free, sugar-free, spice-free, fruit-and-veggie-free, bubble-gum-free. I even tried food-free for a few days. That didn't work either. I just got so weak that when I did one I almost fell over.

Mum says it's because I'm so nervy. The doctor says my digestive process is a victim of stress. The kids at school say I let one out so often I should have an exhaust pipe.

They're right, but I wish they weren't so cruel and unkind about it.

Specially as it's their fault.

Nobody thought my name was hilarious till our new art teacher, Mr Pugh, arrived. At the start of his first lesson he noticed my name on the class list.

'Amazing,' he said, looking around the class. 'Charles Rennie Mackintosh, where are you?'

I put my hand up.

'That's wonderful,' said Mr Pugh, beaming at me. 'You must be named after the legendary early-twentieth-century Scottish furniture design genius.'

I looked at him, puzzled and confused. I'd never even heard of the other Charles Rennie Mackintosh. None of us had.

'No, sir,' I said. 'I'm named after a singer and a dead dog and my dad, sir.'

I explained that Ray Charles is Dad's favourite singer and Rennie was a dog Mum had when she was a kid in Adelaide and Mackintosh is Dad's family name even though we're not Scottish.

Mr Pugh looked a bit puzzled and confused.

Then he spent the rest of the lesson telling us about the other Charles Rennie Mackintosh, who as well as designing furniture also designed plumbing, curtains, pottery, jewellery, rooms, oil paintings, clocks, buildings and cutlery.

Mr Pugh went online and put photos on the whiteboard of Charles Rennie Mackintosh's own house, which is on display in an art gallery in Glasgow. Not the photos, the actual house.

You couldn't see why they'd bother. It was a bit boring. The rooms were all decorated the same, mostly white. And there were little pieces of blue glass stuck in the middle of the doors and bed-heads and kitchen cupboards. It looked a bit mental. I felt sort of embarrassed for both us Charles Rennie Mackintoshes.

Then it happened.

'Your house sucks, Mackintosh,' muttered somebody behind me. 'It looks like a very old iBook.'

Everyone laughed.

I'd never had a whole class laughing at me before.

I went so tense my tummy hurt and before I knew it I'd let one out. A loud one. Which had never happened to me in public before.

Everyone laughed again.

Which made it happen again.

Mr Pugh hardly even noticed. He just told us all to be quiet and carried on showing us pictures of Charles Rennie Mackintosh's very weird furniture. Including very tall chairs with bits of wood missing from their backs on purpose.

'Look,' somebody whispered. 'His chairs have got air holes.'

I glanced around the room. The class were grinning at each other and sniggering at me.

I could see exactly what they were thinking.

Farty-pants chairs.

I don't get the school bus anymore.

It's too stressful with everyone putting on those fake Scottish accents. I'd rather walk. It's only another half hour.

Anyway, Mum's got me on a high-fibre diet at the moment, which means I have to eat these sorghum pellets straight after school and I'd rather do it in private.

Yuk, they taste horrible.

'Charles Rennie Mackintosh,' says a voice behind me. 'Slow down, yeah?'

I turn.

A girl in my class is hurrying towards me. Her name's Jane something. She's hardly ever spoken to me before.

'Alright?' she says.

'I'm in a rush,' I mutter, hurrying away.

She's probably on a dare. A mockery dare.

I glance up and down the street to see if any of the others are hiding in hedges or front gardens.

They don't seem to be.

'I know how you feel, Chas,' she says, catching up and walking next to me.

I give her a look. I doubt she does know, seeing as she hasn't got the same name as a legendary early-twentieth-century Scottish furniture design genius and, to the best of my knowledge, she's never let one off in class.

'I've got a suss name too,' she says. 'Jane Austen, innit.'

I shrug.

'What's so bad about that?' I say.

'Jane Austen,' she says. 'You know.'

I don't know. I've never heard of Jane Austen.

'Story writer,' says Jane. 'Centuries ago. You want classic novels and literature and stuff, she's the business. Mr Bailey says she's well legendary.'

Mr Bailey, our English teacher, is obviously keeping this to himself because he hasn't said anything to the rest of us. I wish Mr Pugh was more like him.

'People gunna get the goss on her one day,' says Jane. 'When they do, I'm knackered.'

She's right. Knowing the kids in our class, she will be.

'Why did your parents call you that?' I say.

'It was my gran in Jamaica,' she says. 'When I was born, my mum was missing Gran so much she let her choose my name. Not clever, eh?'

I shake my head sympathetically.

My parents weren't clever either, it turns out. The thought makes my tummy hurt.

Jane Austen sniffs and wrinkles her nose.

'Was that you?' she says.

'Sorry,' I say, fanning the air behind me. 'What'll you do if people find out about your name?'

'Dunno,' she says. 'They'll probably start dissing me about historic prose styles and satirical subtexts and that.'

I nod. They probably will if they know what those things are. Which I don't. I'm impressed. I've never met a kid before who can talk like Mr Bailey.

'Listen,' says Jane. 'Wanna do a deal? If I look out for you now, will you look out for me if I get sprung?'

I think about this.

'OK,' I say.

She doesn't tell me how she's going to look out for me. Just gives me a thumbs up and heads off.

I feel myself grinning.

There probably isn't anything she can do to help. But it feels good, having Jane Austen watching my back.

By the time I get home I'm exhausted. Sorghum pellets just don't give you the energy for long-distance walking.

'I'm home, Mum,' I yell. 'I'm going up for a snooze.'

I stop at the bottom of the stairs.

Something smells strange. Like wet paint.

'Come in here, Charlie,' calls Mum from the living room.

I go down the hall. But I don't go into the living room straight away. Instead I stare at the door. This morning when I went to school it was just wood. Now it's got little pieces of glass in it, arranged in a pattern. Light is coming through the bits of glass, making them glow.

They're blue.

I think I've seen bits of glass like that somewhere before.

'In here, Charlie,' calls Dad.

That's unusual. They must both have finished work early. Usually they only do that when I have a medical appointment.

I go into the living room. And almost fall over with shock.

Our carpet has gone. So has our wallpaper. The armchairs, dining chairs and TV have gone too.

Everything's white. The whole room. Walls and floorboards. And white armchairs that I've never seen before, weird-shaped ones. Our dining table used to be light brown, but now it's white. Around it are white dining chairs, really tall ones, with bits of wood missing from their backs.

I stare at them.

I know where I've seen chairs like that before.

'What do you think?' says Mum.

She and Dad are standing by the fireplace,

grinning. They've got old clothes on and they're both covered in white paint splotches.

I look around the room again.

I'm gobsmacked. I can't even find the words to tell Mum and Dad how gobsmacked I am.

'We've been planning this for a while,' says Mum. 'Since we found out who Charles Rennie Mackintosh was, and realised we'd put you right in it.'

I don't know what to say.

'That's why I've been spending so much time in the shed,' says Dad.

I've been wondering. I hoped he was inventing underpants that filtered smells, but I thought he was probably just watching football on his very old iBook.

'When we saw how beautiful Charles Rennie Mackintosh's designs are,' says Mum, 'we wanted to show you. So you'll feel better about your name.'

'Thanks,' I say quietly.

I mean it.

I notice a big book on the dining table. On the cover is a photo of Charles Rennie Mackintosh's white living room, like the pictures Mr Pugh showed us.

The book is called *Charles Rennie Mackintosh, Architect, Artist, Icon*. I don't know what an icon is, but I can see he was quite a bit better at it than Mum and Dad.

His living room paint was more of a soft glowing

yellowy-white with no brush hairs stuck in it. His rugs and curtains had beautiful delicate patterns with no paint splotches. And his furniture didn't have a single nail showing.

But I don't care, because what Mum and Dad have done is a very loving thing, plus it must have cost a packet.

'Do you like it?' says Mum.

I nod and give them both a hug.

I wonder if the first Charles Rennie Mackintosh had great parents too.

'Read it?' says Jane Austen, looking suspicious. 'Why?'

I glance around to make sure nobody can see us here behind the bike shelter. I push the library book into her hands.

'So you'll feel better about your name,' I say.

She stares at the book.

'*Pride And Prejudice*,' she says. 'I don't even know what that means, do I?'

'Just give it a try,' I say. 'I've read the intro. It's quite interesting.'

Jane has a sudden thought.

She stares at me, horrified.

'Did you get this from the school library?' she says.

I nod.

'That's it,' she says. 'I'm knackered, innit.'

I know what she's worried about.

'Relax,' I say. 'It's the only Jane Austen book in

the whole library. It hasn't been borrowed for about eight years. Nobody else here has read it. Your secret's safe.'

She looks doubtful.

'I'm not much of a reader,' she mutters. 'I'm well slow.'

'Give it a try,' I say. 'I read a book last night about Charles Rennie Mackintosh, and I'm feeling a bit better already.'

I don't say anything about Mum and Dad redecorating the living room. Jane's mum might not be able to do that. The local council probably won't let you put eighteenth-century Tudor beams in a modern house.

Jane is staring at the book.

'I'll think about it,' she says. 'Ta, anyway.'

In English I let out a big one.

I don't mean to. I never do. They just creep up and then, whoosh, too late.

Everyone sniggers.

We're doing verbs. To teach. To learn. To snigger. Those sorts of words. That's probably what caused it. The stress of knowing exactly what people will mutter if I do one.

They're starting now.

'To woof.'

'To blatt.'

'To fluff.'

'That's enough,' says Mr Bailey in a weary voice

without turning round from the board.

'To fumigate.'

Bang.

There's a sound from the back of the room like a gunshot.

We all turn round.

Jane is sitting at her desk, her hands on the book I gave her. She must have just slammed it down.

She glares at the other kids.

'It is a truth universally acknowledged,' she says, 'that a bunch of idiots who spout the bleeding obvious must be in want of a brain.'

We all stare at her.

We look at Mr Bailey.

Mr Bailey is staring at her too.

Then he grins.

'Well said, Jane,' he chuckles. 'Very well said.'

After Jane looked out for me in class like that, the least I can do is invite her and her mum round to our place for tea.

I explain to Mum and Dad it will have to be Saturday because Jane's mum works late at the video store during the week.

'Jane Austen?' Mum says. 'Like the writer?'

I nod.

'Better have cucumber sandwiches with our chips then,' says Mum with a grin. 'Like they did in the eighteenth century.'

'Good idea,' I say.

Mum sees I'm not joking.

I look forward to it all week.

It's only now I'm realising how it could all turn into a disaster. If Mrs Austen thinks our living room is stupid, and laughs, and I feel embarrassed for Mum and Dad, and my digestive system becomes a victim of stress and . . . I don't want to think about it.

Jane and her mum both blink as they step into our living room.

'Blimey,' says Jane.

'Very striking,' says Mrs Austen.

'It's well white,' says Jane. 'Whitest room I've ever seen. Including most toilets.'

'Jane,' whispers her mum. 'Manners.'

'I'm just saying,' says Jane. 'A truth universally acknowledged, innit.'

I concentrate on keeping my tummy calm.

Dad takes Jane and Mrs Austen's coats.

'Please,' says Mum. 'Sit down.'

We all sit on the white chairs.

I can guess what Mrs Austen is thinking. White chairs aren't very practical. We'll go through gallons of stain remover. I wonder why the Charles Rennie Mackintosh book didn't mention anything about stain remover.

'Nice chairs,' says Mrs Austen.

'Thanks,' says Mum. 'White's our favourite colour.'

She stops and stares awkwardly at Jane and Mrs Austen.

My tummy gives a lurch.

Dad jumps in.

'Cup of tea?' he says.

'Yes please,' says Mrs Austen. 'Oh, before I forget, I made this for you.'

She reaches into her bag and pulls out something and half unwraps it. She hands it to Mum. It's a big round sausage nestling in greaseproof paper.

'Thank you,' says Mum, taking it doubtfully.

'It's a haggis,' says Mrs Austen. 'But you'd know that, being Scottish.'

Mum and Dad glance at each other.

They don't say anything.

'I tell you what's funny,' says Mrs Austen. 'That haggis has almost exactly the same ingredients as an old Jamaican recipe my mother uses.'

'How about that,' says Dad.

'Alas,' says Jane. 'How we humans strive to keep each other at a distance, only for coincidence to undo all our, like, labours.'

While Mum and Dad get busy in the kitchen, I ask Jane how she's going with *Pride And Prejudice*.

'Don't ask,' says Mrs Austen.

'She's a well slow writer to read,' says Jane. 'But her movies are fit. I been watching them all. *Pride And Prejudice* and *Sense And Sensibility* and *Persuasion* and all them. That Jane Austen rocks.'

I give Jane a grin and she gives me one back.

We talk about the eighteenth century for a while, specially how elegantly they used to speak, and then we talk about the early twentieth century, specially how elegantly they used to make furniture, and then Mum and Dad bring in the chips and the cucumber sandwiches and the haggis.

While Mum serves, I feel a high-pressure system building up in my insides. I've never eaten haggis before, and I'm always worried with new food that my exhaust pipe's going to get a serious work-out.

'What's in this?' I say, getting a lump of haggis on my fork.

'The usual,' says Mrs Austen. 'Oats, onions and spices.'

'Mmmm,' says Mum. 'Sounds yummy.'

'And minced sheep's heart,' says Mrs Austen. 'And chopped up lungs and things.'

'I think I'll start with a cucumber sandwich,' says Mum.

Dad does too.

I can't. I've already got a lump of minced sheep's innards on my fork.

Jane and her mum are watching me.

I put it in my mouth and chew.

'How often we fear the strange,' says Jane through a mouthful of chips, 'and find fear itself the only fearful part of it, innit.'

She's right.

Haggis tastes really nice. Nutty, meaty, spicy and sheepy all at once.

50

I love it.

And an amazing thing's happening. My high-pressure system's going away. I eat some more. My insides relax some more. I keep eating. Not a peep, not a whistle.

'Thanks for bringing this,' I say to Mrs Austen.

She gives my hand a squeeze.

'Thought you might like it,' she says. 'What with your name and all.'

She smiles and I notice that her eyes are as blue as the glass in the living-room door. I remember something I read once about the Caribbean, which is where Jamaica is. They have a type of ancient magic there called voodoo, which can kill but it can also heal.

I know I shouldn't be nosy, but I can't stop myself.

'What does your mother do in Jamaica?' I say to Mrs Austen, trying to sound casual. 'Does she have a job or, you know, hobby?'

'Before she retired, she was a lecturer at Kingston University,' says Mrs Austen.

'Really?' says Mum. 'What did she teach?'

'English literature,' says Mrs Austen.

I glance at Jane, who grins and rolls her eyes.

'So I was never gunna get Kylie, was I?' she says. 'Know what I mean?'

'I think Jane Austen's a beautiful name,' says Mum.

'Ta,' says Jane, putting some chips into a cucumber sandwich.

Mrs Austen is still smiling, and looking at me.

'Charles Rennie Mackintosh,' she says. 'That's a nice name too.'

I smile back and have another mouthful of haggis.

I wonder if Jane Austen wrote a book about a person who was universally in need of a friend and got one and ended up much less of a farty-pants.

I'll have to ask her.

Meadows Library

Checkout summary

Name: Aisha Abeyratne
Date: 11/08/2022 14.47

Loaned today

Title: Stink & the world's worst super-
    stinky sneakers
ID: 002849719X
Due back: 01/09/2022

Title: Pizza cake and other funny stories
ID: 002793106X
Due back: 01/09/2022

Title: The Twits /
ID: 002968722X
Due back: 01/09/2022

Title: Judy Moody and the bad luck
    charm
ID: 002974264X
Due back: 01/09/2022

Total item(s) loaned today: 4
Previous Amount Owed: 0.00 GBP
Overdue: 0
Reservation(s) pending: 0
Reservation(s) to collect: 0
Total item(s) on loan 4
For renewals and information
Tel 0151 288 6727

Secret Diary
Of A Dad

Sunday, 3 January

Not a good day.

This morning the kids said to me, 'Dad, why are you kneeling on the floor with your head in the fridge? Have you got a headache?'

I explained I hadn't, I was just telling the plastic salad containers about my school days.

Maddy and Dylan stared at me.

Nine-year-olds and seven-year-olds can be a bit slow sometimes.

'It's one of my New Year resolutions,' I explained, showing them the list I'd made. 'See? Number four.'

'*Spend more time talking to the kids*,' read Maddy.

I took the list back.

'Does it say kids?' I said, peering at it. 'I could have sworn it said lids.'

The kids sighed. So did the lids of the plastic salad containers.

'Pity you haven't kept the first New Year resolution on your list,' said Dylan.

'I have,' I said, showing them the brochure for the package tour I've just booked to the Antarctic. 'See? *Find new glaciers.*'

The kids sighed again. 'Dad,' they groaned, pointing to the list, 'it says *Find new glasses.*'

I squinted at the blurry writing. A chill crept up my spine and not just because I'd left the fridge door open.

'Oh dear,' I said. 'Now I'm feeling a bit worried about New Year resolutions two and three.'

The kids studied the list and found number two. '*Polish the car,*' they read. 'What's wrong with that?'

I took them outside and pointed up to the roof of the house.

'There's no car up there,' said the kids.

Then they saw the shiny cat.

The cat slid off the roof, leaving a trail of wax polish on the tiles. The kids caught it, glared at me and we went inside.

'Number three can't be worse than that,' said Maddy.

I could feel a headache coming on, so I put my head in the fridge again.

The kids read out number three.

'*Get more sleep.* What's so bad about that?'

I closed my eyes, laid my head down next to the lettuce and waited for them to hear the sounds of baaing coming from the living room.

Wednesday, 6 January

I'm feeling very proud today.

Actually, the feeling started a couple of days ago, when I found my glasses and built my first ever piece of furniture. OK, it wasn't perfect, but I did it without help and I was proud of myself. I could feel my chest swelling almost as much as the finger I'd hit with the hammer.

'Well?' I said to the kids when they came to look. 'What do you think?'

I held my breath as they ran their hands over the four sturdy legs, the finely stitched upholstery and the skilfully hung mirrored door.

'Funny-looking bookshelves,' they said.

My chest deflated. They were right. Who was I kidding? I've always been a hopeless handyman.

'Do-it-yourself furniture,' I said bitterly. 'If there's anyone who can actually build this stuff I'd like to know their secret.'

The kids looked at the empty boxes strewn around the room.

'Perhaps, Dad,' said Maddy gently, 'it involves assembling the bookcase, the couch, the coffee table and the bathroom cabinet as four separate items.'

Kids can be know-it-alls sometimes, specially when they're right.

'It was the stupid instructions,' I said. 'They were impossible to understand. Look at that diagram. I broke a screwdriver trying to follow that.'

The kids sighed.

'That's the furniture shop logo,' said Dylan.

I realised what my problem was. I didn't speak the language of do-it-yourself.

I went to my local language school and enrolled.

'Which language would you like to learn?' said the receptionist. 'French? Spanish? Japanese?'

'Furniture Assembly,' I said.

The language teacher tried hard, but by the end of the day I still couldn't translate the phrase '*Slot base-support bracket A into side-panel rib B.*' I couldn't even say it.

'I'm sorry,' said the teacher. 'I can't do any more for you.'

I looked at him pleadingly. 'Not even put my bookshelves together?'

He shook his head.

At home, I stared gloomily at the assembly instruction booklet for the stupid bookshelves. Why could I make other complicated things like sandwiches and hot chocolate with marshmallows, but not a piece of furniture?

Well, no point brooding. Give up and move on.

I stuffed the instruction booklet into the row of books on the bookshelf and turned away.

Hang on.

I turned back.

The bookshelves were built. With base-support brackets slotted into side-panel ribs and everything.

'We did it while you were at the language school,' said Maddy.

'It was actually quite easy,' said Dylan.

I stared at them, amazed. I gave them both a big hug.

Incredible. My own kids can build furniture.

I am so proud.

Tuesday, 12 January

Today on holiday I finally got a chance to take the kids somewhere I've wanted to take them for a long time.

'If you think the green mould down the back of the fridge is amazing,' I said to them, 'wait till you see a rainforest.'

'Mum,' said Maddy, 'are you sure you don't want to come with us?'

'No thanks, my loves,' said Anne, settling down on the motel verandah with a book. 'Have a good time.'

In the car I could see the kids were puzzled how anyone could prefer reading a first-aid book to visiting nature.

I didn't blame them. I didn't get it either. If I had, I would have turned the car round. Instead, I parked it in the rainforest carpark.

'OK,' I whispered to the kids as we crept into the awesome green cathedral of trees and ferns. 'I want you to remember this is a very fragile place. Be gentle and respectful and don't touch anything. Let's just stand absolutely still for a moment and listen to the sound of nature in harmony. Let's appreciate the delicate balance of a beautiful forest unspoiled by the destructive ways of man.'

'I wouldn't stand absolutely still if I was you, Dad,' said Maddy. 'A millipede the size of a comb has just run up your leg.'

I took her advice. I didn't stand still. I ran around in circles beating at my trousers with bracken and rubbing my bottom against several species of tree fern.

'You said we weren't allowed to touch anything,' said Dylan. 'You told us the rainforest is a fragile and delicate ecosystem and touching one leaf could muck it all up.'

'It is,' I said as I whacked at my upper thighs with a cedar log. 'And it could. Which is why I'm trying very hard not to touch any leaves.'

It wasn't easy.

I rolled around on the ground for a while, then reached inside my shirt, rummaged a bit, and pulled out a stag beetle the size of a telephone.

'Don't hurt it,' said the kids. 'And don't wave it around your head like that. You'll give it an upset tummy.'

The beetle finally released my arm from between its mandibles and scuttled away. Weak with relief, I tried to stand up. Something gave way underneath me.

'Dad,' said Dylan, 'do you think you should be sitting in that scorpions' nest?'

I didn't answer. I didn't want to disturb the big scorpion on my tongue.

'Also, Dad,' said Maddy, 'that's a rare stinkhorn fungus you're squashing. That foul-smelling slime is meant to be for the insects, not you.'

I spat the scorpion out and staggered to my feet.

'OK,' I said. 'Let's all calm down. Let's remember we're guests here in this idyllic paradise.'

I reached down to pick up my camera. It wasn't there. A large spider had just eaten it. The spider took a step towards me. It wanted my binoculars.

'Run,' I yelled to the kids.

We ran, crashing through the lush undergrowth. Leeches the size of drinking straws leapt up at us. Fruit-sucking moths the size of fruit swooped down on us. Green pythons the size of green pythons (the big ones) stuck their tongues out at us.

'Wow,' said the kids. 'You didn't tell us rainforests were this exciting.'

Exhausted, dripping with sweat and the rather unpleasant substance that double-eyed fig-parrots exude from their bottoms, I collapsed onto a large moss-covered rock.

The rock moved. It was a giant tree frog looking for a tree that could support its weight.

'Arghhh,' I yelled. 'Please, don't hurt us, we're a protected species.'

We ran again. I led the way, sinking into swamps, struggling with giant ferns, wrestling my way past orchids that kept giving me karate kicks.

The kids stayed on the walking track.

Finally we reached the carpark.

I hugged the car with relief for a while, then took a deep breath and turned to the kids.

'Well,' I said, 'there you have it. The tropical rainforest, nature's most precious gift to the planet.'

'And,' said Maddy, 'her most threatened one.'

Dylan nodded in agreement.

'You're right,' I said. 'Even as we stand here, watching my ankles being nibbled by Herbert River ringtail possums, rainforests all over the world are being burned, chopped, mulched and bulldozed.'

The kids looked at me.

'We agree those things are awful, Dad,' said Maddy. 'But they're definitely not the biggest threat to rainforests.'

I didn't understand what she meant.

The kids opened the car and made me sit inside it with a book. Then they went back into the rainforest without me.

Saturday, 16 January

Normally we all feel a bit down in the dumps at the end of a holiday, but not today. We're all very excited.

We've just got our first dog.

She arrived this morning. I think I was even more excited than the kids. The confusion. The noise. The joyful howls (the dog). The puddles on the carpet (me).

'Don't worry,' I said. 'It's only tea. Come on, we've got a dog to look after.'

I'd read all the dog-care manuals, so I knew exactly what to do first.

Give her a feed.

'Better let us do that, Dad,' said the kids, taking the bowl. 'Better safe than sorry.'

I was indignant. The dog was indignant.

'Why?' I demanded.

'Because,' whispered Maddy so the dog wouldn't hear, 'you're hopeless with pets.'

I was deeply hurt.

'That goldfish,' I retorted, 'died of a bad cold.'

The kids looked at me sternly.

'It died,' said Dylan, 'because of what you fed it.'

I was even more indignant.

'The box had pictures of fish on it,' I said. 'How was I to know it was cat food?'

The kids looked sad. The dog looked nervous.

I took her for a walk round the block.

'We'll do that,' called the kids, running to catch up. 'Better safe than sorry.'

I boiled with indignation. The dog tried to hand them the lead.

'You're not being fair,' I said. 'I've never had a single accident taking a dog for a walk round the block. Or a fruit bat. Or a blue-tongue lizard.'

'That's right,' said Dylan sadly. 'Just a mouse. What on earth possessed you to throw that stick and tell our mouse to fetch it?'

'With a hungry cat on the loose,' said Maddy. 'Whose dinner you'd just fed to the goldfish.'

Before I could answer, I realised I was holding an empty lead.

The dog had disappeared.

We found her up a tree, trembling with fear.

The kids managed to coax her down, but only after I'd made a promise. That when I enrol the dog in training and obedience classes, I'll enrol as well. Ten weeks for the dog, twelve for me.

Sunday, 17 January

I try to be a good dad, but there are some skills I just don't have. Like watching TV while I'm being stared at. Specially by a dog with a lead in her mouth and two kids with cricket bats in theirs.

'Dad,' said the kids, 'you promised you'd take us to the park.'

'Wmpf,' agreed the dog.

'Please don't talk with your mouths full,' I said. 'I promised we'd go after I've finished watching *The Bill*.'

'But Dad,' they wailed, 'we thought you meant one episode on telly, not two hundred and eighty-seven episodes on DVD.'

I sighed.

'Please,' I said. 'I'm trying to concentrate.'

I turned back to episode fifteen. Or was it sixteen? This was criminal.

'We'll go after I've finished watching *The Bill*,' I said firmly, 'and nothing you can say will make me change my mind.'

'Suit yourself,' said the kids. 'But if you don't get any exercise, you'll die.'

It was pouring with rain in the park, but I didn't care because I took a brilliant diving catch.

'Howzat!' I yelled through the mud.

The umpire shook her head.

'Wmpf,' she said, licking her bottom.

On the way home I decided there must be a way to combine telly and exercise and mud-free nostrils.

That night I experimented.

'Who wants a lolly?' I asked, tossing one up and swinging my table-tennis bat.

It was a big success with the kids. They're such quick learners. When I told them they could have dinner in front of the TV, they just sat there with their mouths open so I could lob the rissoles in with a squash racket and whack the peas in with a golf club.

'Let him, Mum,' they squealed happily. 'It's exercise.'

My dear wife rolled her eyes in that loving way of hers. And later in the evening, when I tried to feed the dog and sliced my shot with the pool cue and put a can of dog food through the TV screen in the middle of episode nineteen of *The Bill*, she smiled approvingly.

Thursday, 21 January

Our new goldfish arrived yesterday. And our new telly. We all sat down and watched the news.

There was a report about how most men let their wives buy their clothes because they have no idea about fashion.

The family were looking at me and nodding. Which was unfair.

'I spilt sauce on my shirt at lunch,' I said. 'That's the only reason I'm wearing this green garbage bag.'

Today I decided to show them I do know about fashion. So I went shopping and bought myself a shirt. A very fashionable colourful bright one.

'Absolutely you, sir,' said the menswear assistant, putting on a second pair of sunglasses.

I squinted at my reflection. I looked like I'd just staggered out of an explosion in a paint factory.

'Are you sure?' I said.

'Computer screens have got millions of colours, right?' said the assistant. 'Well, this shirt's got even more millions. Definitely suits you, sir. The greens match your complexion.'

I wore it home. Cars swerved, buses ran into each other, and a light plane made a forced landing dragged down by the temporarily blinded birds clinging to its wings.

Not really. As if one shirt could cause a reaction like that.

Except at our place.

When I walked in, the whole family dived for cover, including the dog.

'Dad,' winced the kids, shielding their eyes

with thick metal baking trays. 'Take it off. All the neighbours are closing their curtains.'

Patiently I explained why I needed to leave the shirt on. I was going to their school tonight for a parent–teacher meeting, and I was worried the teachers would lose interest and start chatting among themselves.

'Bright colours grab people's attention,' I said. 'Look at fire engines, and The Wiggles.'

'Dad,' sighed the kids, shielding the goldfish's eyes with lolly wrappers. 'When our teachers cop an eyeful of that shirt, they won't be giving you attention, they'll be giving you detention.'

'Rubbish,' I said. 'Teachers are tough, specially around the eyeballs.'

I was right. At school tonight I had the teachers' attention from the moment I walked in.

'So,' I said to Dylan's class teacher. 'How's Dylan doing with maths?'

She just kept staring at the shirt. Her lips were moving, and for a second I thought she was answering my question, but she wasn't.

'One million,' she was murmuring. 'Two million, three million . . .'

Saturday, 23 January

The judge looked at me sternly. 'Today,' he said, 'you have been charged with one of the most serious crimes ever to be tried in this courtroom. How do you plead?'

The public gallery was packed and the jury was staring at me accusingly. My mouth felt like a sandpit in the Simpson Desert.

'Not guilty,' I croaked. 'I'm innocent. I didn't do it. Honest.'

The prosecutor was on her feet. 'I put it to you,' she said, 'that on the fourteenth of November last, at bedtime, you read your children *The Twits* by Roald Dahl and that you wilfully and intentionally left out the bit about the wormy spaghetti because you didn't want to miss the start of the footy on telly.'

'Not true,' I cried. 'It wasn't footy, it was netball.'

The jury stared at me without blinking. Stuffed toys can be very stern.

I put my head in my hands.

'All right,' I moaned, 'I admit it. I couldn't bear to read all of *The Twits* again. I'd read it 127 times in the past year.'

My son took the witness stand.

'That wasn't the worst example,' he said to the prosecutor. 'In July, Dad read us *War And Peace* and all we got was, Once upon a time there was a war, and then there was peace, the end.'

'I couldn't stand it again,' I moaned. 'Not for the eleventh time.'

'And was that,' said the prosecutor to her brother, 'the same week he read us *Ode To A Nightingale* by the very famous English poet John Keats?'

Dylan looked at her sadly. 'He said it was Keats,

but we just didn't think that, Tweet tweet OK kids time to settle down now *The Bill*'s started, sounded much like a classic poem.'

It was a long trial.

I was found guilty.

While the main witness for the prosecution returned to his judge's chair and put his fluffy toilet-seat-cover wig back on, I looked pleadingly at the jury for mercy.

Nothing.

The jury foreman, who'd taken her prosecutor's dressing gown off, explained to me that the jury was pushing for a long sentence, except for one of the fluffy pink teddies, who wanted death.

Fortunately the judge didn't agree.

He sentenced me to nineteen years' hard labour.

I knew what that meant. Nineteen years' hard labour each night before bedtime.

I groaned and reached for *The Twits*.

Sunday, 24 January

I've always encouraged the kids to stand up for what they know is right, and I'm pleased to say I think I've succeeded.

Take today for example.

'We want you to promise,' the kids said to me this morning, 'to look after our polluted planet and not make any more unnecessary trips in the car.'

'I promise,' I said.

They opened the boot and let me out.

'Because let's face it, Dad,' said Maddy, 'you are very lazy when it comes to walking.'

'Not any more,' I protested. 'This week I did the supermarket shopping on foot.'

'Only partly,' said Dylan. 'You got exhausted between Frozen Foods and Breakfast Cereals and hitched a ride on someone's trolley.'

Kids, they don't miss anything.

'OK,' I said. 'But on Friday I went to the dentist on foot.'

'Part of the way,' said Maddy. 'We had to carry you the last fifty metres, as usual.'

I gave a sigh. Which turned into a gasp when the kids said they wanted us to do our trip to the museum today by public transport.

'By leaving the car at home and taking the train,' said Maddy, 'we'll be reducing our consumption of scarce fossil fuels and our emission of harmful gases.'

I think that's what she said. I'd locked myself in the car after the word 'train'.

'It's not a long drive,' I mouthed through the windscreen. 'Just a couple of litres of unleaded.'

Using hand signals and the karaoke amplifier, the kids reminded me about our previous car trip into the city. After driving there (2.3 litres), we'd looked for a parking spot (19.7 litres). Failing to find one, we'd parked on the footpath (8.6 litres – it was a high kerb). We'd returned from the museum to find a parking ticket on the car (5.2 litres attending court to dispute the fine, 164 litres getting the car back from Bundaberg after it was stolen from outside the courtroom).

The kids had made their point.

We were on the platform in plenty of time for the 12.15 train to the city. So were lots of other families with environmentally stubborn kids like mine.

A metallic voice crackled above us.

'The 12.15 train to the city is running eighty-seven minutes late due to running into the back of the 11.47 which was running thirty-one minutes late due to the driver being late to work due to the trains running late.'

I took a deep breath.

Boy, it's not easy treating our planet with care and respect. I still haven't forgotten the fiasco with our new solar hot-water system. I mean, where in the owner's manual does it say, Don't put block-out cream on the solar panels?

On the platform the kids made a pensioner squeeze up on a bench so I could sit down.

'Try and relax, Dad,' they said. 'Getting angry and breathing heavily increases your carbon output and contributes to global warming.'

The 11.28 arrived soon after one o'clock and we travelled into town.

At the museum there was an old train on display. I asked the staff if it could be returned to service, possibly at 12.15 each day. They explained it was too old. They said they were, however, expecting a newer train which had been donated last year but which was running thirty-seven weeks late.

When we arrived at the city station for the trip home, the platform was packed. The train arrived on time. Applause broke out. The kids told me to stop as I was the only one doing it.

'See?' they said. 'Public transport isn't so bad.'

Then we noticed that the train had only half the usual number of carriages.

'We always run smaller trains on the weekend,' said a railway employee as he disappeared under the surging mob.

We were packed in like sardines in a really small bit of ocean.

The kids didn't mind, but I was thin-lipped the entire trip home. I tried not to be, but I had someone's umbrella hooked into one corner of my mouth and someone else's two-year-old hooked into the other.

We managed to struggle off the train three stops past ours. We made it back to the station carpark before midnight. The car had been stolen.

I'm writing this while I wait for the train to Bundaberg.

It's running thirty-eight minutes late.

Luckily the kids aren't here to check my breathing.

Can't Complain

As soon as the waiter put Petal's plate on the table in front of her, Petal knew that breakfast was going to turn ugly.

The mushrooms were sliced.

Piffle, thought Petal.

It wasn't fair. The eggs were perfect, the bacon was brilliant, the sausage was dandy and the tomato was tops. You could see why this was Mum and Dad's favourite cafe.

It was just the mushrooms.

Petal glanced at Mum and Dad. Maybe she could eat the mushrooms very quickly, before Mum and Dad noticed them. It was possible. Dad was busy on his phone, complaining to a clothing manufacturer that the label on his underpants was too scratchy. Mum was on her phone too, texting a complaint to the neighbours about their squeaky garage door.

Petal grabbed her fork.

Too late.

'Those mushrooms are sliced,' said Mum, frowning. 'You asked for them not sliced.'

'It doesn't matter,' said Petal. 'Honest.'

'The waiter asked if you wanted them sliced or not sliced,' said Mum. 'And you said not sliced.'

'I just said that because he asked,' said Petal. 'I don't mind, really.'

Dad put his phone down.

'I'll send them back,' he said.

'No,' said Mum. 'I think Petal should do it.'

Dad thought about this and nodded.

'Mum's right,' he said to Petal. 'You should send them back.'

Petal sighed.

Coming to a cafe for a cooked breakfast was meant to be a school holiday treat, but this wasn't feeling like a treat any more.

'Please,' said Petal. 'It's OK. I like mushrooms sliced or not sliced. I don't mind how they're done.'

Mum sighed. So did Dad.

'Petal,' said Mum. 'You've got to stop this ridiculous everything's-OK-in-the-world attitude. Everything's not OK, and the world won't improve until more people speak up. You've got to start complaining more, Petal.'

Petal wanted to complain now.

She wanted to complain to Mum and Dad that they were making her life a misery with their non-stop complaining. She wanted to tell them that the world would be much more OK if it wasn't full of people getting cross and arguing and fighting. And complaining about mushrooms.

But she didn't.

Mum and Dad always won arguments. And then complained about how Petal wasn't very good at arguing.

The waiter came over nervously with Mum and Dad's breakfasts.

'Two fried eggs,' he said as he put Dad's plate down. 'Free-range, no salt, yolks up, cooked for one minute forty seconds in grape seed oil not butter.'

Dad peered suspiciously at his plate.

The waiter put Mum's plate down.

'Herb omelette, one and a half eggs,' he said. 'Thirty-five grams of cheese, five grams of parsley, no chives, no dill. With linseed and buckwheat toast, medium rare.'

'That's not five grams of parsley,' said Mum.

The waiter looked like a man hearing exactly the bad news he was dreading.

'It must have been a bit damp when the chef weighed it,' he said. 'Here, I brought extra just in case.'

Petal wanted to crawl under the table and stuff French loaves in her ears. Instead she watched as the waiter held out a small plastic container of chopped parsley and Mum took a pinch.

'Hang on,' said Dad. 'What's that plastic container made of?'

The waiter looked at Dad in alarm.

'Plastic,' he said.

Dad took the container and turned it over. Chopped parsley fell onto the table. People at other tables were watching. Petal tried to look like she was only with Mum and Dad because she'd been kidnapped and taken out for a cooked breakfast against her will.

'See that recycling number?' said Dad to the waiter, pointing to the bottom of the container. 'Number seven. That means the plastic's made with polyethyldextrose hexachloride, which latest studies show gets into food and builds up in the human body.'

Particularly in the human brain, thought Petal, looking at Dad wearily.

'It's just a plastic pot,' stammered the waiter. 'We use them all the time.'

'Do the health inspectors know you use them?' said Mum.

'I'm sure they do,' said the waiter miserably. 'They've been here four times this year, remember? After you complained to them about the chipped plate, the squeaky chairs, the size of our salt grains and the taste of our tap water.'

'Well if they know about this,' said Dad, handing the container back to the waiter, 'and if they haven't done anything, it's a disgrace. When we've finished our meal, I'm going over to the council offices to complain.'

Petal sighed.

Breakfast at home would have been so much simpler. Except Mum had a complaint in to Kelloggs. Something about their rice bubbles making too much noise.

'How's your meal?' said the waiter to Petal.

'Lovely, thanks,' said Petal. 'I really like the mushrooms.'

After breakfast, Petal followed Mum and Dad over to the council offices.

'Can I wait outside?' she said.

'No,' said Mum. 'This is part of your education. We want you to grow up to be an assertive consumer and a citizen who stands up for her rights.'

What about my right to a quiet life, thought Petal as she followed them in. And everyone's right to a peaceful world.

'Is there anything else we need to complain about while we're here?' said Dad.

Mum had a ponder.

'Noisy leaf blowers in their parks,' she said.

'Good thinking,' said Dad.

Good grief, thought Petal. We'll be here all day.

Soon Mum and Dad were in an argument with the council officer at the service counter. Petal tried to find a spot behind Mum and Dad where they'd think she was hearing everything, but where she wouldn't have to listen to them.

'. . . chemically-impregnated parsley,' she heard Dad say to the man.

Petal took a step back. Two more steps and she'd be behind the ornamental fountain in the council foyer. Then she wouldn't have to watch them either.

'Petal,' said Mum. 'Pay attention.'

Wearily, Petal took half a step closer.

'. . . United Nations declaration of human rights,' she heard Dad say.

Then Petal noticed two other people in the foyer, sitting on a bench. A woman in a big dark-coloured Arabic dress. It looked a bit like a dress Mum had bought online and then complained that the website had got the sizes wrong.

The woman's head was covered by a scarf, but her face was uncovered and Petal could see she was crying.

A girl was with her. The girl looked about the same age as Petal, and her hair was covered too. She was trying to comfort the woman.

Petal went over.

'Excuse me,' she said to them. 'Are you alright?'

The woman shook her head.

'Thank you,' she said. 'But is no good.'

She sobbed some more.

Petal looked at the girl, who was hugging the woman. She looked close to tears herself.

'Can I get someone to help you?' said Petal.

The girl scowled.

'They won't help,' she said.

She held out a printed piece of paper. Petal saw the words *Camera Parking Infringement Notice*.

'One hundred and seventeen dollars,' said the girl. 'For something we didn't do.'

Petal saw that next to *Offence* was written *Stopped in a loading zone.*

'With council cameras you can ask for photos,' said Petal. 'They have to give you a photo to prove you did it.'

Mum and Dad had asked the council for photos heaps of times. They'd done it last week to prove that parking near the bottle shop made your car extra dirty because everyone braked heavily when they saw the specials of the week and sprayed out extra brake-lining dust.

'We've got photos,' said the girl.

She held out another sheet of paper.

Printed on it were fuzzy black-and-white images of a battered old car in a loading zone parking space.

'Is that your car?' Petal asked the girl.

The girl nodded.

'Is not justice,' sobbed the woman.

Petal wasn't sure what to say next. The photos showed their car was in a loading zone, which Petal knew was just for trucks and vans. They didn't have a leg to stand on as Dad said recently in the chicken shop when he was complaining that the drumsticks were too fatty.

'It was that day last month with very heavy rain,' said the girl.

Petal remembered the day. A massive storm had swept across the city. Lashing rain and huge hailstones that piled up in drifts. Nobody had seen anything like it in summer before. It just happened without any warning. Afterwards Mum complained to the TV weather people.

'We drove through a flood,' said the girl.

Petal remembered the flood. She and Mum and Dad had driven through it near the supermarket. Dad complained to the Roads And Traffic Authority about their drains not being big enough. Or their phone complaints call centre.

'We couldn't see the road properly,' said the girl. 'So we pulled over. The rain was so heavy, at first we didn't see we were in a loading zone. As soon as we realised, we drove away. We were there for one minute and a half, but the camera saw us.'

Petal peered at the photos. One showed the car driving into the loading zone. It had a time on it. *15:42:16.* The next photo showed the car driving off. The time on that was *15:43:45.*

Frowning with effort, Petal did the calculation. And kept frowning as she realised the girl was right.

One minute twenty-nine seconds.

A hundred and seventeen dollars.

In blinding rain.

'Have you told this to the council?' said Petal.

The woman and the girl both nodded.

'They said if we don't pay, we must go to court,' said the girl. 'We can't afford to pay. My mother works cleaning offices at night and her wages are really low.'

Petal stared at the photos again.

A quiet life was one thing, but this wasn't fair.

'Petal,' called Mum crossly.

Petal glanced over. Dad was showing something on his phone to the man at the counter. A list of chemicals found in plastic, probably. Or in parsley.

'What are you doing, Petal?' said Mum. 'I want you over here listening to this.'

Petal turned back to the girl and pointed to the pieces of paper.

'Can I show my parents?' she said. 'I think they might be able to help. They're very good at complaining.'

The girl and her mother looked at each other. They both nodded to Petal. The girl handed over the sheets of paper.

'Thank you,' said the girl's mother.

Petal went back to the counter.

'. . . if the council wants to use leaf blowers,' Dad was saying to the man, 'ratepayers should be issued with earplugs.'

'Mum,' whispered Petal. 'Those people over there need help. They're victims of a heartless council camera. Can you and Dad complain for them?'

Mum looked at the papers Petal was holding.

She sighed.

'Petal,' she said. 'This is exactly what we've been trying to get through to you. If you don't learn to stand up for yourself, you'll be a victim all your life. Like those people.'

'But will you help them?' said Petal.

Mum sighed again.

'Helping them wouldn't really be helping them,' she said. 'How are they going to learn to stand up for themselves if other people do all their complaining for them?'

Petal tried to point out that the girl and her mother had already complained, but Mum wasn't listening.

'It's the same with you, Petal,' said Mum. 'You have to stop hiding behind other people. You have to start standing up for what you believe in.'

Alright, thought Petal grimly. I will.

She stepped over to the counter.

Dad was in the middle of telling the council officer some statistics about leaf-blower-related hearing loss.

'Excuse me, Dad,' said Petal.

Dad stopped, surprised.

Petal looked sternly at the council officer.

'I want to complain,' she said. 'People shouldn't be fined for taking refuge in a storm.'

The council officer looked at Petal.

He glanced at the papers she was holding.

'Roads And Traffic Act, paragraph one seven nine, subsection three,' he said. 'Passenger vehicle stopped in loading zone. Their appeal has been rejected.'

'That's not fair,' said Petal. 'There was hail up to people's knees. It was on the news.'

'Roads And Traffic Act, paragraph one seven nine, subsection three,' said the man again.

Petal showed the man the times on the photos, and how smoke was coming out of the car's exhaust pipe in all of them.

'They were only there for one minute twenty-nine seconds,' she said. 'Look, they didn't even turn their engine off.'

'Roads And Traffic Act, paragraph one seven nine,' said the man. 'Subsection three.'

Petal was about to thump her fist down on the counter, but before she could, Dad stepped in.

'Hey,' he said to the man. 'Give her a break. It's her first time.'

The man didn't look impressed.

Before Petal could say anything else, she was steered away from the counter. Mum was holding one arm, Dad the other.

They were both gazing at her in delight.

'That was wonderful,' said Mum.

'Well done, love,' said Dad.

'But he wouldn't listen,' said Petal.

'Don't worry,' said Mum. 'It happens a lot. You'll get used to it. But it was a very good start. We're proud of you.'

Petal didn't feel proud of herself.

'Pop over and give the lady her documents back,' said Dad. 'We're almost finished here. I just need to have another word to this bloke about airborne particles near bottle shops.'

Petal went back over to the girl and her mother. They were both looking hopeful.

'How'd you go?' said the girl.

Petal started to say not very well. But something in their faces stopped her.

'I haven't finished yet,' she said to the girl. 'But you'd better get your mum home. Things could turn a bit ugly here.'

When Petal came out of the toilet, Mum and Dad were still arguing with the man at the counter.

'...and what's more,' Dad was saying, 'brake dust gets spread even further by leaf blowers.'

Petal walked carefully to the centre of the foyer and climbed up onto the ornamental fountain. She climbed carefully because she didn't want the toilet rolls under her t-shirt to fall out.

Once she was up there and had found her balance, she faced the counter.

'Attention council officers,' she said in her loudest voice. 'I have toilet rolls taped to my body.'

This wasn't completely true because she didn't have any sticky tape, but she carried on, hoping her bluff would work.

'If you don't give in to my demands,' she said, 'my mum and dad will take photos of me on their phones and email them to the media. Everyone will see them and wonder why a person would stick six toilet rolls up their t-shirt in public. They'll think, if people have to do that to get this council to listen to them, this council must be really slack.'

Petal paused for breath.

She glanced at Mum and Dad. They were looking a bit slack themselves. Around the mouth. Petal hoped the council gave in to her demands, because Mum and Dad didn't look like they'd be taking many photos. Not if they stayed in shock like that.

'Here are my demands,' said Petal loudly. 'One, nobody gets fined for spending less than two minutes in a loading zone in bad weather. Two, all the council's cameras get painted a bright colour so we can see where they are. Three, people who pay office cleaners really low wages are not allowed to use the library. Four –'

But Petal didn't get to deliver her fourth demand because Mum and Dad grabbed her and yanked her off the fountain and hurried her towards the door.

'Are you crazy?' muttered Mum, pulling a toilet roll from under Petal's t-shirt. 'What if people thought this was a bomb?'

'I'd have blown my nose on it to show them it wasn't,' said Petal. 'But they noticed me, which is the most important thing when you're complaining, right?'

Mum and Dad didn't say anything.

They grabbed the rest of the toilet rolls, left them in a pile just inside the door, and hurried Petal out into the street.

Dad kept glancing nervously over his shoulder to see if they were being followed.

'That was a good start,' said Petal. 'But we need to do more. I promised the lady and her daughter I would.'

She felt in her pocket to make sure she still had their phone number.

'I think it'd be safer if you just write a letter to the local paper,' said Dad.

'I'm planning to,' said Petal. 'But first let's go to the hardware store and get some chains and padlocks, and chain ourselves to a loading zone sign.'

Mum and Dad glanced at each other with worried faces as they hurried Petal towards the car.

Petal wondered if they were going off the idea of complaining. That would be a shame, because she was just getting a taste for it.

After all, thought Petal. They did show me how to do it, so they really can't complain.

Draclia

Corey woke up suddenly.

It was dark. At first he wasn't sure where he was. In his ear a squeaky voice was hissing something about blood.

Corey tensed. He could just make out a shadowy figure looming over him, pressing him into the pillow. A figure with big staring eyes and white teeth.

Corey didn't panic.

He waited till he could see better.

Yes, it was just as he'd feared. He was being pinned to the bed by a five-year-old boy in dinosaur pyjamas clutching a plastic truck.

'Will,' groaned Corey. 'You're kneeling on my neck.'

'It's got her,' squeaked Will. 'In the front yard. A vampire's got Shelley and it's eating her blood.'

Corey closed his eyes. Maybe he was still asleep.

Maybe if he tried really hard, he could go back to his dream about the ice-cream cake Mum and Dad got him last week for his birthday. Three delicious flavours in the shape of a footy stadium.

'If you don't wake up,' said Will, 'I'll tell Mum how you stayed in bed and let a vampire get Shelley while she was supposed to be babysitting us.'

Corey groaned again.

He got up. He didn't have any choice. Will was dragging him by his bottom lip.

They stumbled to the window.

Will wrestled open the curtain. Corey helped him. Will pointed down into the front yard.

'See?'

Corey squinted. Mostly he could just see shadows. Then the moonlight went brighter and he saw Shelley leaning against the side of the carport.

Somebody was with her. Another teenager.

Corey shuddered. It was a fairly yukky sight. Shelley had her arms wrapped around the teenager, and the teenager's mouth was on her neck.

'I think it's Draclia,' whispered Will, his breath hot in Corey's ear.

Corey sighed.

'The word is Dracula,' he said. 'And that's not Dracula down there, it's Jarrod Bennet.'

Will didn't look convinced.

'Jarrod Bennet's in high school with Shelley,' said Corey. 'His younger sister Brianna goes to our school.'

Will thought about this.

'Does Brianna know her brother's a vampire who bites people on the neck?' asked Will.

Corey sat down wearily on his bed.

'Jarrod is Shelley's boyfriend,' he said. 'They've been going out for nearly a week.'

Corey tried to explain to Will that Shelley and Jarrod were just kissing. And that because Shelley was very tall for her age, Jarrod couldn't reach her lips, not even on tiptoe, and so he had to make do with her neck.

Will still didn't look convinced.

Corey realised it was all probably a bit technical for a five-year-old.

'I saw it on telly,' said Will. 'Vampires don't care if they're short cause they've got big teeth.'

Corey sighed again.

You couldn't really blame a little kid. Not in a world gone vampire mad. There had hardly been a day in Will's young life without a new vampire movie being released or a new vampire romance book being published or a new vampire TV show being launched or a new vampire burger being advertised on the car radio.

Little kids noticed things like that.

It had been the same for Corey when he was small and the world had been dinosaur mad. For a few weeks when he was five, Corey had seriously suspected there were dinosaurs trapped in the ice under the frozen peas in Coles.

Corey made Will sit next to him on the bed.

'Vampires are just stories,' he said to Will.

His little brother shook his head. He jumped up onto Corey's lap. Corey could smell something weird on Will's breath.

'Vampires live among us,' muttered Will darkly. 'Shelley told me.'

Thanks Shelley, thought Corey. I hope I'm that thoughtful and considerate when I'm fifteen.

'Why does your breath pong?' he said as he lifted Will down.

'It's garlic butter,' said Will. 'I went downstairs and had some. To stop Jarrod Bennet biting me.'

Corey looked at the clock.

Ten past ten. Mum and Dad probably wouldn't be back from book club till eleven.

Corey needed sleep now. Desperately.

But he knew there was only one way he was going to get it.

'OK,' he said to Will. 'Come on. I'll prove to you that vampires are just stories.'

Shelley's room was full of vampires.

But, as Corey carefully pointed out to Will, none of them were real.

Shelley had about a hundred vampire romance story books and DVDs on her shelves. Plus posters of hunky heart-throb teenage vampire guys, and plastic models of them, and a *Twilight* bedcover.

'See,' said Corey. 'Vampires are just pretend.'

'Mum's got heaps of gardening books,' said Will, 'and gardening's real.'

Corey took a deep breath.

'Look,' he said, 'even if there was such a thing as vampires, which there isn't, Shelley wouldn't go out with one. She can be a bit bossy at times, but she's not stupid.'

'She would so go out with one,' said Will. 'She told me. She likes vampire boyfriends. All her friends do.'

Corey stared at the *Twilight* bedcover.

It's all that movie's fault, he thought bitterly. I wish I had the phone numbers of the people who made up that movie and all those books. I'd make them come round and stay up half the night arguing with Will, so I could get some sleep.

'Anyway,' said Will, 'Draclia makes you be his girlfriend. I saw it on a cartoon.'

Corey opened his mouth to remind Will that (a) information from cartoons isn't that reliable and (b) the word is Dracula.

Before he could, Shelley burst into the room.

'What are you doing in here?' she said, glaring at them.

'Um,' said Corey. 'We couldn't sleep.'

'Out,' said Shelley.

'We've come to save you,' said Will. 'From Draclia.'

Shelley rolled her eyes angrily and gave Corey a 'grow up' look. Which Corey felt was very unfair as he was grown up, almost. Will was the little kid with the dopey ideas.

'I was just trying to explain something to Will,' said Corey. 'He's got some dopey idea about Jarrod. Of course it's completely –'

Corey didn't finish. Shelley grabbed the front of his pyjama top and twisted it so tight he could hardly breathe.

'Stay away from Jarrod,' she hissed, eyes blazing. 'If you do anything to upset him, you're dead meat, both of you.'

Even though his brain was struggling for oxygen, and he was concerned about Will who looked close to tears, Corey was still able to work out almost instantly why Shelley was being so emotional.

It was her height.

Teenage boys didn't like teenage girls who were taller than them, not as girlfriends. Shelley had said that tearfully to Mum a million times.

But now, at last, she'd found one who didn't mind. So of course she didn't want him driven away by a loony five-year-old vampire hunter and a not-very-good-babysitter brother.

Corey could understand that.

The thing he couldn't understand, now Shelley had pulled him even closer for a glare and he could see her skin in more detail, was why she had blood smeared on her neck.

'Corey, wake up. Corey, wake up. Wake up, Corey.'

Corey woke up.

Will's face was touching his. It was sticky. Corey

could smell milk and cornflakes and truck plastic and just a hint of garlic.

'Draclia's in the kitchen,' whispered Will urgently.

Corey closed his eyes. The early morning sunlight was hurting his head. So was Will's voice. For a moment he wondered if Will was a vampire. A sleep vampire who took all your sleep.

'In *our* kitchen,' said Will, even more urgently.

'Go and keep him busy,' mumbled Corey. 'Show him your truck. Don't let him leave. And don't say anything about vampires. I'll be down soon.'

'OK,' said Will, and hurried off.

Corey was tempted to go back to sleep. But he didn't. He had to fix this once and for all. Put Will's mind at rest. So life could go back to normal.

In the shower Corey made a list in his mind of all the things he knew about vampires.

1. They hate sunlight.
2. They hate having wooden stakes stuck in them.
3. They hate garlic.
4. Sometimes they can turn into bats.

Right, thought Corey as he went down to the kitchen. I must be able to use at least one of these to prove to Will that Jarrod Bennet is not a vampire.

Mum and Dad and Will were at the kitchen table.

Nobody else was.

'Where's Shelley?' asked Corey casually. 'And, um, Jarrod?'

'Don't know,' said Dad. 'They were here a moment ago, then they just sort of vanished.'

'Shelley wouldn't let me show Draclia my truck,' said Will bitterly.

Corey sighed. Will was glaring at the chair Jarrod must have been sitting in. Which was empty now except for a cricket bat.

A cricket bat?

Corey stared at the bat, mind racing.

Could vampires turn into that sort of bat?

He shook the thought away and told himself to stop being silly. This wasn't helping anyone.

'I think they've gone to the mall,' said Mum.

'Strange one, that Jarrod,' said Dad. 'I asked him if he wanted to watch me play in the over-forties cricket, but he wasn't interested.'

'Yes he was, love,' said Mum. 'But he's got very sensitive skin. He doesn't like being in the sun.'

Corey told his imagination to calm down. Lots of people had sensitive skin. Babies, for example.

Could babies be vampires?

Corey took a deep breath. This sort of wild thinking wasn't getting him anywhere. Next he'd be wondering if goldfish could be vampires.

What I have to do, thought Corey, is be more scientific.

'Got any plans today, Corey?' said Mum.

'Um,' said Corey. 'I'm going to Brianna Bennet's house to do a scientific experiment. I can take Will if you like. I think he'll be interested.'

'Yes,' shrieked Will. 'I love scientific speriments. I'm a vampire for scientific speriments.'

'The Bennets live next to the cemetery, right?' said Dad.

Corey nodded.

'Go the long way round the block,' said Mum. 'So you don't have to cross any roads.'

Corey nodded again.

He was only half listening.

Mostly he was wondering if Mum had any garlic butter left.

'Why don't we just ring the bell?' said Will.

Corey dragged Will back down into the bushes.

'Because,' whispered Corey, 'we can't just stand at the front door and say, hello Mrs Bennet, we've come to hide a lump of garlic butter in Jarrod's bed to prove he's not a vampire, and, by the way, could you let us know if he starts foaming at the mouth or writhing around on the floor or not being able to concentrate on his homework.'

'Why can't we?' said Will.

Corey took a deep breath.

He decided to keep it simple.

'Because,' he said, 'it's more fun to climb in through Jarrod's bedroom window.'

'Yes,' shrieked Will, or would have done if he hadn't been muffled by the hand Corey slapped over his mouth.

Luckily the Bennets' house was single storey,

and Jarrod's room was easy to spot. Shelley had been telling everyone for days that Jarrod had black curtains.

What Shelley hadn't told anyone, Corey discovered, was that Jarrod also had a really sharp flyscreen that cut your finger when you pulled it off the window.

'Ow,' said Corey, sucking his finger.

'Don't let it bleed,' said Will. 'If Jarrod smells your blood he'll go into a frenzy and want to marry you.'

Corey didn't think there was a huge chance of that happening.

He concentrated on sliding Jarrod's window open as quietly as he could, then helping Will climb through. It took a while because Will had his school backpack on, which got wedged in the window.

Corey muttered some cross things very quietly and pushed as hard as he could. Suddenly Will and the backpack tumbled forward onto Jarrod's bed. Corey climbed through after him.

'Why did you bring your backpack?' he whispered, helping Will off the bed. 'You don't need your truck for vampire hunting.'

'It's not my truck,' said Will indignantly. 'It's a stake.'

Corey stared at him.

'A stake for vampire hunting,' said Will. 'If you jab a stake into a vampire, they –'

'I know,' said Corey hurriedly.

He was shocked that Will even knew about this, let alone was planning to do it. And where had he got the stake anyway?

Corey slid the backpack off Will's back.

Best if I look after it, he thought. That's all we need now, a five-year-old running riot with a piece of sharp wood.

Then Corey saw something and froze.

Blood was dripping from the bottom of the backpack onto Jarrod's floor.

Corey stared, horrified.

Had the stake already been used?

Frantically he fumbled with the backpack zip, jerked it open and pulled out what was inside.

A torn plastic bag with raw meat in it.

'I told you,' said Will. 'It's a steak. I got it from the fridge at home. If you jab a steak into a vampire it distracts them and –'

'Not a steak,' said Corey weakly. 'A stake.'

'That's right,' said Will. 'A steak.'

'Jarrod, is that you?' called a grown-up voice outside the door.

Corey froze again. He gave Will a pleading look to make him stay still. He tried to stay completely still himself. Which wasn't easy because he had blood trickling along his arm.

The door opened.

Mrs Bennet put her head in and stared, surprised.

'Hello,' she said.

'Hello,' said Corey weakly.

Mrs Bennet stared at him some more.

'You're Shelley's brother, right?' she said.

Corey nodded. He could see she was looking at the dripping steak in his hand.

He tried to work out how he was going to explain to Mrs Bennet (1) why he and Will were in her son's bedroom doing a vampire hunt, and (2) why they were doing it in such a stupid way.

'Oh, silly me,' said Mrs Bennet, suddenly smiling. 'Of course. Jarrod must have invited you over for a bite.'

Will gave a terrified squeak.

Corey swallowed nervously.

'Your mum needn't have bothered with this,' said Mrs Bennet warmly, taking the meat from Corey. 'My husband always gets too much steak for our barbecues. Come on through, lunch is nearly ready. Brianna and the others will be pleased to see you.'

Dazed, Corey grabbed Will's hand as Mrs Bennet steered them out to the back patio.

'Look who's here,' said Mrs Bennet to the people sitting around the table.

Everyone turned and stared at Corey and Will.

Mr Bennet and Brianna looked surprised, but pleased as well.

Jarrod just looked surprised.

Shelley looked cross.

'They even brought their own meat,' said Mrs Bennet.

Nobody else said anything. They were all looking a bit puzzled and lost for words.

Corey decided he should say something.

'And our own garlic butter,' he said.

At first it was quite a tense barbecue.

Particularly for Will. Corey could see he was extremely tense, glancing nervously at Jarrod. Shelley looked very tense too, glancing nervously at Corey and Will.

Corey decided to help everyone relax.

'Vampires,' he said. 'You can't get away from them these days, can you?'

Everyone looked a bit startled at first.

Corey had to hold Will's hand tight under the table to keep him there.

But soon everyone was talking about their favourite vampire movies and TV shows and books. Even Shelley started to relax.

Corey chose his moment.

'Sorry we broke into your room, Jarrod,' he said.

'My room?' said Jarrod, looking surprised again.

'Will wanted to get to know you better,' said Corey. 'Now you're one of the family. Lucky your bed was there to break our fall. And lucky it's a strong bed. With strong bedsprings. In your bed.'

He hoped he'd said it enough for Will to get the message.

'That bed needs to be strong,' said Mrs Bennet. 'The number of hours Jarrod sleeps.'

Thank you, said Corey silently.

'Twelve hours a night, if they let him,' said Brianna.

Thank you as well, said Corey silently again.

'Easy to see Jarrod's not a vampire,' he said out loud.

Everyone looked at Corey.

Corey realised he hadn't explained enough.

'Vampires don't need beds,' he said. 'They don't sleep. Not ever. Not even on long trips in the back of cars.'

Everyone laughed. Including Shelley. And when Corey glanced across at Will, he was grinning too.

Corey felt light-headed with relief.

Problem solved. Except for one little nagging thing. The blood he'd seen on Shelley's neck. If Jarrod wasn't a vampire, how did it get there?

Corey wondered if Shelley had cooked dinner yesterday evening and maybe had tucked the meat under her chin so she'd have both hands free to chop onions.

It was possible, except last night they'd had fish and chips.

'OK, time to eat,' said Mrs Bennet. 'Jarrod, get rid of that revolting gum, please.'

Jarrod stuck something on the edge of his plate.

Red bubblegum.

Corey stared at it.

Of course. The red smears on Shelley's neck. It wasn't blood, it was bubble-gum juice.

Corey felt happier than he had for ages. Happy

that Shelley had managed to find a boyfriend at last. Happy that Jarrod's family were so nice and friendly and mortal. Happy that with a bit of luck Will would stop carrying on like an insomniac Transylvanian innkeeper and let him get some sleep.

Then Mr Bennet brought the steaks over from the barbecue.

Corey stared.

They were barely cooked. The outsides were sort of scorched, but the insides were still red.

'We always have our steak rare,' said Mr Bennet. 'Hope you like it that way.'

Mrs Bennet plonked a steak on Corey's plate.

'There you go,' she said. 'Folk who climb in through windows have to keep their strength up.'

Corey felt faint.

He hadn't even cut his steak yet, and a puddle of blood was trickling out of it. What could he do? Everyone thought he and Will had come to lunch. You couldn't come to lunch and not eat the lunch.

Corey cut off a small piece of steak. He tried not to look at the blood. He put the piece of steak into his mouth and hoped he wouldn't throw up.

He didn't.

The steak was delicious.

He had another piece.

This was incredible. It looked revolting but tasted fantastic. The mixture of crisp burnt outside and tender juicy inside was the best thing he'd ever tasted that wasn't in the shape of a footy stadium.

Corey had more.

Then he remembered Will. He turned to his brother.

Will was eating even faster than Corey. His eyes were shining as he chewed. He grinned at Corey, lips red and gleaming.

Corey grinned back.

He looked around the table. Everyone was eating as enthusiastically as Will.

'Good, eh?' said Mr Bennet.

Everyone nodded, mouths full.

Corey put another big tender dripping chunk of meat into his mouth and chewed happily.

Then he had another little nagging thought and stopped.

Was this how it all began? The taste for blood. Centuries ago. Before anyone had ever bitten anyone else in the neck. Was the first vampire just someone who'd been to a really good barbecue?

Corey smiled to himself.

Don't be silly.

But he hesitated.

Then he reached over to the garlic butter and cut off a dollop and smeared it over the rest of his steak before he put the next big chunk into his mouth.

Just in case.

Tickled Onions

I hate doing this, but every morning I have to.

The other kids call it Clyde Craddock's mental moment.

As soon as I arrive at school, I hurry over to the garbage bins behind the canteen. First I check the bins for leftover bread from yesterday, because by 8.45 in the morning I'm always starving.

There's usually a slice or two. I wipe off the soggy lettuce or coffee powder or pencil sharpenings and gobble it down.

Then, meal finished, I get busy with the other thing I have to do.

I pull the plastic bag out of my pocket, careful not to spill what's inside it. Cold porridge, maybe, with stewed apple and sun-dried tomatoes. Or a sour plum and leek yoghurt pancake. Or goat sausages with pig-liver marmalade. Or whatever else we had for breakfast at our place.

I always feel guilty as I dump my breakfast in the bin, because I know it was cooked with love. Mum and Dad are the most loving parents in the world. They're just not that good at cooking.

Or listening.

After I've dumped my breakfast, I take my lunch box from my school bag, open the lid carefully, try not to breathe in the revolting smell, and dump my lunch too.

Today's smell is even worse than usual.

It's partly the salami-mousse sandwich, which is one of Mum's favourites. But mostly it's the tickled onions.

That's what Dad calls them, and I suppose he's allowed to because he invented them. They're like regular pickled onions except for the rose petals and chilli powder and fermented fish paste.

Into the garbage they go.

Some of the kids from my class are watching me and giggling.

'Mental,' I hear a couple of them whisper as usual.

I sigh as usual.

I don't really mind. Not that much. I'm used to it. I've been doing this since year one and we're in year six now.

But I live in hope that one day I'll hear the other kids whisper something else. Something like, 'Poor Clyde, it must be really hard for him, having parents whose hobby is amateur cooking.'

I'd really like that.

Oh well, at least my morning routine isn't as bad as Hamish Hodge's. At least I don't have to actually eat this muck. Not like poor Hamish.

Here he comes now, with Rick, Jock, Mick, Jack and Vic.

I hate this. They're twisting Hamish's arms even further up his back than they usually do.

I wish they'd grow up. Most of us year sixes are in the footy club or the movie club or the phone club. But Rick, Jock, Mick, Jack and Vic had to be different. They had to start a club called Overweight Watchers. A whole club just to make fun of overweight people.

'Hodge Podge coming through,' the club members are chanting like they do every morning. 'Starving fat boy hasn't eaten for ten minutes. Needs to see what's on the breakfast menu.'

This is usually when I turn away.

It's not just the horrible sight of Hamish having his head forced into a bin. It's the look he usually gives me before it happens. A look that says, 'If only you'd eat your breakfast, I wouldn't have to.'

But today I'm not turning away.

I'm taking a couple of steps towards Rick, Jock, Mick, Jack and Vic.

'Hey,' I say. 'Lay off him.'

What's going on? Hunger must be scrambling my brain and giving me the powerful desire to spend a couple of weeks in hospital hooked up to a drip.

Rick, Jock, Mick, Jack and Vic are glaring at me. They're all big, specially Vic who does weightlifting as part of her netball training.

I'm quite tall, but I don't have much meat on my bones. It's not really surprising, seeing as I live on one meal a day from the bins, plus whatever sandwiches I can get from people for doing their homework.

'Creepy Craddock's being a hero,' says Jock, narrowing his eyes at me. 'Risking his neck for Hodge Podge. I didn't know you two were friends.'

Hamish Hodge is looking at me as well, eyes wide and confused because we're not friends. Other expressions twitch onto his plump face. He's hoping I'll save him. He's also worrying I'll make things worse.

I started this, so I have to finish it. Dad says it's important to finish what you start, though he's usually talking about food.

'Yeah, me and Hamish are good friends,' I say to Jock. 'I'm going to his place for dinner tonight.'

I hadn't planned to say that, but now I have, it sounds like quite a good idea.

Rick, Jock, Mick, Jack and Vic are looking surprised.

So is Hamish.

Then all the others smirk.

'I'd like to see that,' says Vic. 'A loony who chucks his food in the bin having dinner with a fatso who can't stop eating.'

They all have a big laugh.

Until Jock stops and gets serious.

'And why exactly should we lay off Hodge Podge?' he says, sticking his face close to mine. 'Is it cause you're gunna make us?'

Jock's breath smells of bacon. I feel faint with hunger. But I manage to remember what I need to say.

I look Jock right in the eyes.

'PD project,' I say.

Jock frowns. Rick, Mick, Jack and Vic glance at each other. Slowly they realise what I mean.

Yesterday Ms Dunphy set a really difficult Personal Development project. It's on Empathy. Four hundred words on Other People's Feelings, by next Tuesday.

'If you let Hamish go,' I say to Rick, Jock, Mick, Jack and Vic, 'I'll help you with it.'

Jock thinks about this.

'If we let the fat boy go,' he says, 'we're not giving you sandwiches as well.'

'Deal,' I say.

The Overweight Watchers club members look at each other, nod, scowl at me, scowl at Hamish, and wander away.

Hamish is panting with relief.

'Thanks,' he says. 'I thought I was going to have to eat those stinky horrible onions again.'

He remembers where the onions come from.

'Sorry,' he says.

'That's OK,' I say. 'You can make it up to me with a delicious meal tonight.'

Hamish stares at me, alarmed.

'Were you serious about coming to dinner?' he says.

'Of course,' I say. 'I don't joke about food. Food is the most important thing in my life. I haven't had a decent meal since I was four.'

While we walk to his place after school, Hamish tells me a bit about himself. We've never really had a chance to talk much. He's only been at the school eight months and he's spent a lot of that time with his head in a bin.

'I wasn't always porky,' he says. 'I used to be almost as skinny as you.'

'What happened?' I say.

I heard somewhere that thyroid glands, whatever they are, can sometimes make people fat. Probably depends how they're cooked.

'My mum died,' says Hamish.

I give him a sympathetic look. It's moments like this you realise food isn't the most important thing.

Not quite.

'My dad's in charge of meals now,' says Hamish gloomily. 'He likes huge meals. Every day.'

This sounds promising.

'What's for tea tonight?' I say.

'Dunno,' says Hamish. 'Could be anything.'

I smile.

Anything, sure, but I'm pretty confident it won't be seafood sausages with pig-liver marmalade.

Hamish's house is nice. Bit like ours, but tidier.

As we come in, a man's voice calls out.

'Nearly finished, Hamie. Get yourself a snack.'

We go into the kitchen. Hamish explains that his dad is a freelance journalist who works at home. I nod, but I'm not fully paying attention. I've just noticed something that's making me feel nervous.

There's no food in the kitchen.

In our kitchen there are jars and packets stacked everywhere, and stuff hanging up all over the place. Chillies and herbs and bits of dried goat. It's all yuk, but there's heaps of it.

Here, nothing.

Hamish opens the fridge and takes out a bottle of water.

I peek in while the door's open. I see some old fruit, half a packet of cheese and a jar of vegemite.

Where are the huge meals?

'Hi there, Hamie,' says Hamish's dad behind us. 'Who's this?'

Hamish's dad is exactly the same shape as Hamish. Not blubbery or anything, but happily plump. I'd like to be that shape.

'Clyde's my best friend at school,' says Hamish.

I try to look as though I am. Which isn't that hard because I don't think Hamish has got any other friends.

'Can Clyde eat with us tonight?' Hamish says to his dad.

Mr Hodge looks me up and down.

'Looks like he needs to,' he chuckles. 'We're going to a steakhouse. That OK with you, Clyde?'

I nod so hard I get giddy.

'Right-oh then,' says Mr Hodge. 'Let's give your folks a call.'

I can't believe it.

This steakhouse menu is amazing.

Most of the steaks are half a kilo at least. And this place obviously hasn't even heard of pig-liver marmalade.

The only thing I'm a bit worried about is the prices. I don't want to send Mr Hodge broke.

Mr Hodge looks up from his menu.

'OK, boys,' he says. 'What are you having? Anything you like.'

I glance uncertainly across the table at Hamish.

'It's OK,' says Hamish quietly. 'The magazine's paying.'

I'm not sure what he means.

'My dad does restaurant reviews,' explains Hamish. 'Two a week for a magazine, plus five for their website.'

'Seven restaurants a week,' says Mr Hodge. He grins. 'Lucky there are seven dinnertimes a week. And lucky I've got a hungry son to help me.'

'Yeah,' says Hamish miserably. 'Very lucky.'

'I'm also writing a book,' says Mr Hodge. '*One Thousand And One Restaurants You Must Visit Before You Diet.*'

Hamish rolls his eyes.

'Only joking,' says Mr Hodge. 'Now, what do you like the look of?'

'Um,' I say, trying not to speak too fast, 'can I have the eight hundred and fifty gram Ridiculously Rotund Rump, please?'

'You sure can,' says Mr Hodge. 'I'm having the Ludicrously Large Lamb Fillet, so, Hamie, would you mind having the Colossal Kilo T-Bone so you can tell me what it's like?'

Hamish nods unhappily. I can see he's wondering how much plumper he'll be in the morning. And whether Rick, Jock, Nick, Jack and Vic will notice.

Hamish's dad is studying the menu again.

'Right,' says Mr Hodge. 'We need to have a starter each, two if you can manage it. And lots of side serves. Fries, onion rings, wedges, nachos. OK?'

Hamish doesn't say anything, so I answer for us both.

'OK,' I say, grinning.

'Thanks for last night,' says Hamish the next morning.

I look up from the garbage bin, where I'm dumping a bag of scrambled eggs. The smell of the sardines and the raspberry vinegar in the eggs is making my eyes water, so I can't see Hamish, but

I assume he's being sarcastic. It must be awful, not enjoying eating in restaurants.

My eyes clear and, to my surprise, Hamish is looking grateful.

I'm glad. I'm feeling grateful too.

'Thank you,' I say to Hamish. 'It was the best meal of my life.'

'Dunno how you did it,' says Hamish, 'eating all the side serves and three desserts and half my T-bone as well as your steak, but thanks.'

'My pleasure,' I say, opening my lunchbox and tossing a dried-goat-and-curdled-whey sourdough sandwich into the bin.

A shadow falls over us.

Five shadows, actually.

Before Rick, Jock, Mick, Jack and Vic can get started on Hamish, I reach into my bag and pull out a sheet of paper.

'I've done you some project notes,' I say. 'Just some basic stuff about other people's feelings, what they are, how they work, how to spot them, stuff like that.'

I hold the sheet of paper out to them. Rick, Jock, Mick, Jack and Vic huddle around and peer at it.

'I'll do some more tomorrow,' I say.

The weight-mocking club glare at me. They glare at Hamish. They're probably feeling a bit stressed at the sight of Hamish with his head not in a bin. But Jock snatches the sheet of paper and they leave.

Hamish is looking at me. I can see there's

something he wants to say. I assume it's another thank you, but it turns out to be something slightly different.

'Clyde,' he says. 'Do you want to have dinner with us again tonight?'

'Good word, "yummy", very good,' says Mr Hodge, opening his notebook on the restaurant table and jotting my word down. 'I don't use that word enough. What about the roast chicken? How would you describe that?'

I think of a different word because I figure that's what a journalist would want.

'Delish,' I say.

'Good,' says Mr Hodge, writing again. 'What about you, Hamie?'

'I didn't have any chicken, Dad,' says Hamish.

'No problem,' says Mr Hodge. 'The lamb chops?'

'I didn't have any of those either,' says Hamish.

I did, the lamb chops were yummy, but now I'm struggling to come up with a new word.

'Lambent,' I say.

I don't know what that means, but Mr Hodges smiles and writes it down.

I describe the fish as 'crunchiferous', the veggies as 'snaporific' and the apple tart as 'crustulant'.

'Good on you, Clyde,' says Mr Hodge. 'You're the perfect professional dining companion. And well done, Hamie, for making such a spot-on best friend.'

'You're welcome,' says Hamish quietly.

Mr Hodge looks at me.

'If I have a word with your parents,' he says, 'would you like to eat with us every night?'

I hesitate for a moment. Only because I'm a bit worried about our dog, Garnish. Usually I take him for a walk each evening so I can slip him my dinner. He's missed out for the last two nights. All he's had is the regular dog food Mum gives him. But now I think about it, he's probably better off. Look how much happier Hamish is now he doesn't have to eat so much.

'Thank you,' I say to Mr Hodge. 'I'd like that heaps.'

'Right-oh,' says Mr Hodge. 'I'll call your folks later. Now I need to go and check out the toilets. A restaurant reviewer's work is never done.'

After his dad has gone, Hamish gives a big sigh.

'Don't worry,' I say. 'I don't have to eat with you every night. Not every single night. You can have your dad to yourself sometimes.'

I already have a plan. If I bring a couple of my plastic bags with me when I do eat with Hamish and his dad, I can stock up for the nights I don't.

'It's not that,' says Hamish. 'I really like having you here. I'm very grateful for how much of my food you eat. I've lost two kilos in the last two days.'

I'm puzzled. Hamish looks like he's about to cry.

'I just hate having a dad who's a restaurant reviewer,' says Hamish. 'I just wish we could eat at home. Normal meals like a normal family.'

I stare at Hamish. I can't believe what I'm hearing. Hamish is like a lottery winner who wishes he hadn't bought the ticket.

'We've been doing this for so long,' says Hamish, 'I think my dad's forgotten what a normal meal at home is.'

Hamish hesitates. He has that look people get when there's something they want to ask but they're not sure how. Even before he spits it out, I guess what it is.

Oh no.

'Clyde,' says Hamish, 'will you invite me and my dad to your place for dinner one night? So he can see how normal people do it. So when I ask him to give up his job he'll understand.'

I open my mouth to tell Hamish what a really bad idea that is. How only an idiot would ask a dad to give up the best job in the world. And how dinner at my place is about as far from normal as you can get without going into outer space and eating radioactive broccoli.

But I don't say it.

Maybe it's Hamish's miserable face, or maybe it's Ms Dunphy's Other People's Feelings project, but suddenly I'm putting myself in Hamish's shoes.

No normal meals.

No mum.

Body shape a whole club has been formed to mock.

Only one friend in the whole world.

And even though the chicken and fish and lamb in my tummy have turned themselves into an anxiety burger, I invite Hamish and his dad to dinner at our place.

'Come in,' says Mum with a big smile a couple of nights later. 'You must be Hamish.'

I introduce Hamish and Mr Hodge to Mum and Dad and Garnish.

We all go into the lounge.

'Peanut?' says Dad, once we're all sitting down.

My tummy goes tense. But it's OK, Mum and Dad are sticking to what they promised. No home-roasted peanuts with curried prawn paste and fermented kelp. Just normal ones with salt out of a supermarket packet.

'Thanks,' says Mr Hodge, taking a handful.

This is going well so far. Mr Hodge likes normal peanuts. If we can give him a whole normal meal, Hamish might get his wish.

I try to concentrate on how good that will be for Hamish. I try not to think about all the restaurant meals I'm going to miss out on.

Hamish loves the peanuts. Well, peanut. He only takes one.

'Crisp?' says Dad.

I go tense again, but it's still OK. They're normal crisps out of a crinkly packet. Normal flavour, not even a hint of intestine.

It's amazing. I gave up trying to make Mum and

Dad listen to me years ago. But yesterday, when I explained to them why tonight had to be normal, they actually heard me. I don't know how I did it. Maybe when you're trying to help a friend in desperate need, you get more determined.

I'll have to suggest that to Ms Dunphy as an idea for a project.

Anyway, Mum and Dad are doing really well.

We're having a nice normal evening.

So far.

'Let's eat,' says Mum.

OK, that's not so normal. I don't think hostesses normally herd guests towards the dinner table only four minutes after they arrive. I think Mum must be feeling a bit stressed by the effort of serving a normal meal.

We go into the kitchen. Our dining table has been in the kitchen for years. Mum and Dad like to have it close to the stove because a lot of what they cook congeals very quickly.

I glance anxiously around the kitchen. It looks fairly normal. Everything's been packed away in cupboards, or under our beds. Except for the dried goat strips, which are hanging in my wardrobe.

'Hope you like roast lamb, Charles,' says Mum to Mr Hodge.

'I do, thanks,' he says.

He looks like he's enjoying himself. He's not quite as enthusiastic as when he's reading a restaurant menu, but he looks pretty happy.

Hamish is starting to glow with happiness.

Mum takes dinner out of the oven. It's exactly what she said. Normal roast lamb. No stuffing, no crust, no bone marrow sauce with pickled fungus.

Dad carves. With a normal knife.

Mum puts the veggies on the table. Roast spuds. Peas. Carrots. Orange ones. Normal shape. No honey mixed in with them. Or bees.

I have a moment of anxiety about the gravy. But it's OK. It's out of a packet.

'Mmmm,' says Mr Hodge. 'That looks amazing.'

I grin at Hamish. He grins back.

We're both about to have the best meal of our lives.

Then I notice that the thing Mr Hodge is staring at, the thing he just said was amazing, isn't the lamb. Or the veggies.

He's looking up at the shelf over the fridge. At the one thing, I now see, that me and Mum and Dad forgot to pack away.

A jar of tickled onions.

'What unusual onions,' says Mr Hodge.

I'm not surprised he says that. You don't often see onions that have turned purple.

Mr Hodge gets up and goes over to the shelf.

'May I?' he says.

Mum and Dad don't say anything. Are they feeling panicked like me? I haven't got a clue what their thoughts are right now, or their feelings, and I've done a project on the subject.

Mr Hodge lifts the jar down, unscrews the lid, takes out a tickled onion, and puts it into his mouth.

Hamish is looking worried too.

I try to calm down. I tell myself that one unusual food item doesn't stop a meal from being normal.

'Incredible,' says Mr Hodge when he's finished crunching the tickled onion. 'Fermented fish paste, right? And chilli. And rose petals. Where did you get these delicious onions?'

Mum and Dad look at each other.

I can see exactly what they're feeling now. Even Rick, Jock, Mick, Jack and Vic could spot this much pride.

'We made them,' said Mum.

'Amazing,' says Mr Hodge.

'We're quite keen amateur cooks,' says Dad.

He opens the fridge and before I can stop anyone, Mr Hodge is tasting pig-liver marmalade and jellied goat-curd tarts and a whole lot of other stuff, with Garnish panting hopefully at his feet.

Mr Hodge looks like he's having the best night of his life.

'What is this incredibly delicious thing I'm eating now?' he says.

'Salami mousse,' says Mum.

Mr Hodge sits back down at the table, deep in thought. He thinks for quite a while. I wonder if he's thinking about why on earth anyone would make mousse out of salami.

Probably not.

I wonder if he's thinking about whether he can come here for dinner every night, which would mean giving up reviewing restaurants and making Hamish eat three meals at a time.

I hope so.

Then Mr Hodge speaks, gazing at Mum and Dad, his eyes shining.

'Stephanie,' he says. 'Neil. Have you ever thought of opening a restaurant?'

There's a stunned silence.

Except for the soft sound of Hamish's sob.

'Come on, boys, your tucker's on the table.'

Me and Hamish don't need to be told twice. We dump our ping-pong bats and dash to the dinner table.

Yum. Veggie soup.

Mrs Walsh is the best housekeeper in the world and she makes the best veggie soup in the world. Her secret is she puts bits of grilled steak in it.

Hamish tucks in. Since Mum and Dad and Mr Hodge opened their restaurant, and Mr Hodge hired Mrs Walsh to take care of his house, Hamish looks forward to dinner at home every night.

So do I. Hamish always invites me.

'Dad's here,' says Hamish happily as a car door slams.

Each evening Mr Hodge comes home from the restaurant for an hour to have dinner with Hamish.

That's only fair, because Mum and Dad have breakfast with me each morning. They don't need to be at Tickled Onions, which is what their restaurant is called, until the first deliveries arrive at ten. Though sometimes the pig livers are delivered earlier.

'Is that veggie soup?' says Mr Hodge, joining us at the table. 'Delish. I'll have a large serving, thanks Mrs Walsh. It's soup, so it's not fattening.'

We all grin.

Mr Hodge has trimmed down a bit since he became a waiter. He reckons he walks twenty kilometres on a typical night in the restaurant. Twenty-five if lots of customers ask for extra pig-liver marmalade.

Hamish reckons he and his dad and me will all be the same shape soon.

It's possible, though modern science reckons body shape is partly the result of body chemistry, as I explained to Rick, Jock, Mick, Jack and Vic in the Personal Development project notes I gave them this morning.

The project is on Violence. My notes explained that violence is sometimes the result of body chemistry too, and that sometimes violent people have to change their diet. I included a recipe for sour plum and leek yoghurt pancakes.

At first Rick, Jock, Mick, Jack and Vic didn't want the notes.

They were more interested in having what was in

my lunch box. I think they could smell Mrs Walsh's pickled onions. But I was hanging on to those.

Mrs Walsh makes them the normal way, and they're delicious.

Stationery Is Never Stationary

'**C**ome on, both of you,' said Mum. 'We'll be late. Jack, switch that game off and get your shoes on. If we don't leave soon, it won't be worth going.'

It's never worth going, thought Jack gloomily. Big family get-togethers should be banned.

While he tied his shoes, Jack imagined a world without Christmas, Easter, birthdays, engagements, weddings, babies, anniversaries, funerals, public holidays, exam results, holiday videos, new houses, overseas trips, footy grand finals and hearing about people's operations.

Heaven.

Because that would be a world where big families wouldn't have any reason to get together. And innocent dads wouldn't feel like losers just because of their jobs.

'Amazing,' said Dad, still on the couch gazing at

his laptop. 'There's a company in Japan that makes teflon-coated staples.'

'Archie,' Mum said to him, her voice loud with exasperation. 'We'll be late.'

'Do we have to go?' said Jack to Mum, like he always did.

'Yes,' said Mum, like she always did. 'Uncle Pete wants us all to see his new home entertainment set-up. Plus it's Aunty Sue's birthday tomorrow, my cousin Niall's just back from Venezuela, Aunty Anthea wants us to meet her new boyfriend and we have to talk about where we're going to have Christmas. Archie, if you don't switch that computer off, I'll brain you with it.'

In the car on the way there, Jack felt miserable like he always did when he and Mum and Dad got together with the rest of the family.

Then he made a vow.

This time he'd try even harder. This time he'd do it. This time he'd make the rest of the family respect Dad's job.

In the driver's seat, Dad turned to Mum.

'You know what this means,' he said.

'What?' said Mum.

'That crowd in Japan must have a staple remover that can handle teflon,' said Dad.

'Concentrate on the road,' said Mum.

Jack concentrated on being determined and hopeful.

He was ten now and he was sure he could do it.

Simple, really.

All he had to do was make Uncle Pete and the others understand that working in a stationery shop was one of the most important jobs in the world.

Uncle Pete opened the front door, his big suntanned face beaming.

'The slack mob have arrived,' he called over his shoulder.

'We're only a few minutes late,' said Mum.

'Doesn't matter,' said Uncle Pete. 'We're just glad you're here. We've run out of paperclips.'

Uncle Pete clearly thought this was hilarious.

Jack thought about taking Uncle Pete to Japan, so Uncle Pete could discover the advantages of teflon-coated staples. In particular how they're less painful when someone staples your mouth shut.

He decided not to.

Give me half an hour, said Jack silently to Uncle Pete, and you'll be gazing at Dad with new respect.

Dad was gazing at Uncle Pete with a nervous smile. Mum was rolling her eyes.

'Thought you top barristers were meant to be witty and original,' she said, kissing Uncle Pete on the cheek.

'I don't do original on weekends,' said Uncle Pete. 'This lot can't afford it. I save it for the people who pay me six grand a day. Probably the same with you, eh, Archie. You probably don't bring your best manila folders home on weekends.'

'Not often,' said Dad. 'Though actually these days the best folders are made from hot-milled cellulose.'

The rest of the family were around the pool. They raised their glasses to Mum and Dad and Jack.

'Rob's just telling us about the hospital he's building in Africa,' said Uncle Pete.

'I'm not actually building it myself,' said Uncle Rob modestly. 'Just arranging the finance.'

Jack waited patiently while Uncle Rob spent the next ten minutes telling them exactly how. Finally he finished. Before Jack could get started with what he wanted to say, Aunty Anthea butted in.

'Rakesh is a digital microchip designer,' she said, giving her new boyfriend a squeeze. 'He's just had a fantastic breakthrough. He's invented a microchip that can be inserted into bananas on trees, and when each banana gets ripe, it sends a text to the farmer.'

Everyone murmured in an impressed way.

Rakesh shrugged modestly.

Jack opened his mouth to say his piece, but Uncle Pete spoke first.

'What about mangoes?' he said to Rakesh. 'I love mangoes.'

'I'm working on that,' said Rakesh.

Everyone murmured again, in an even more impressed way.

'The plum industry in Venezuela's been having a few problems,' said Mum's cousin Niall before Jack could get a word in. 'That's why I was over there. Helping them eradicate the sap-sucking fruit moth. We did it with genetic modification. Quite easy really, but don't tell that to the Nobel Prize committee.'

'South American fruit industry,' said Aunty Sue, snapping her fingers. 'Didn't you have something to do with that, Pete?'

Say no, begged Jack silently.

Uncle Pete shrugged even more modestly than Rakesh had.

'Just helped out a few of the growers,' he said. 'Twenty thousand indigenous Impala people from the northern rainforests. They were being victimized by an oil company who wanted them off their land.'

'How terrible,' said Mum.

'Oil company was burning their homes,' said Uncle Pete. 'Plus it wouldn't accept their supermarket discount coupons at petrol stations. I got it all sorted out for them in the International Court of Justice.'

Everyone murmured in a glad sort of way.

Except Jack. He was starting to feel weak and defeated, like he always did at big family get-togethers.

It was happening again.

He couldn't even get a word in.

'Saw you interviewing the prime minister on telly,' said Aunty Sue to Mum. 'Good job.'

Mum shrugged modestly.

At least when Mum looks modest, thought Jack, she means it.

'What about you,' said Mum to Aunty Sue. 'Heard on the grapevine they want you to run that new university in Singapore.'

Aunty Sue gave a wry smile.

'Can't see it happening,' she said. 'They want me to stay on as Vice-Chancellor of the uni here as well. I'd be flying up and down every second day.'

'Come on,' said Aunty Anthea. 'Get real. I'm the chairman of Qantas. I can get you discount fares.'

Everyone laughed fondly.

Except Jack, who felt like pushing everyone into the pool.

'What about you, Archie?' said Uncle Pete to Dad. 'What's new for you at work?'

Jack had been dreading this. He felt sick.

Dad thought for a moment, chewing his lip. Then his face brightened.

'There's a very interesting range of non-toxic highlighters that's just come in,' he said. 'Oh, and we've finally found some price labels that don't leave sticky marks on the pens.'

There was a long silence.

Jack watched in agony as the others just looked at Dad.

It was now or never.

'Dad saved several hundred lives last week,' said Jack.

Everybody looked at Jack, surprised. And puzzled. And clearly not believing him.

Specially Dad.

'It's true,' said Jack. 'Don't be modest, Dad. Tell them how many notebooks you sold last week.'

Still puzzled, Dad had a think.

'Ten maybe,' he said. 'And quite a few post-its.'

'There you go,' said Jack. 'Imagine how many disasters would've happened if those people hadn't been able to write themselves notes. *Remember to turn the gas off.* There's a few houses blown up for a start. *Feed the dog.* Pets can turn really nasty when their blood-sugar level drops. *Don't leave the chainsaw where the kids can play with it.* See what I mean?'

Jack looked around at the staring family members.

They didn't seem to see what he meant.

'Sticky tape,' he said desperately. 'Imagine what would happen if people's glasses snapped while they were driving and they didn't have sticky tape. Carnage on the roads.'

Uncle Pete and the others were starting to frown and glance at Mum and Dad.

Jack kept going.

'Pens with sparkly ink,' he said. 'They can prevent wars. If the leaders of two countries are having a border dispute, a birthday card signed in sparkly ink can make all the difference.'

Mum put her arm on Jack's shoulder.

'That's enough, love,' she said. 'It's a good point, but you've made it.'

Jack could see from everyone's faces that he hadn't made it very well.

Even Dad didn't look convinced.

'Bit of advice, Jack,' said Uncle Pete. 'From the legal world. You're talking about things that haven't happened. People don't care about things that haven't happened.'

Aunty Sue and the others nodded.

Jack went into the house.

You're wrong, Uncle Pete, he thought. People can care a lot about things that haven't happened. For example, there's an important thing that hasn't happened right now. Nobody's patting Dad on the back and saying 'Wow, Archie, we hadn't realised how important and interesting your job is.' That definitely hasn't happened.

Jack glanced out the window, just to make sure.

Nope, not happening.

'Wow, Pete,' said Aunty Anthea. 'We hadn't realised how expensive and impressive your new home entertainment set-up is.'

The rest of the family murmured in agreement.

Uncle Pete grinned proudly.

Jack, who'd followed the family down the steps, had to admit it was impressive. A room specially excavated under Uncle Pete's house with a massive

TV screen and a pile of high-tech equipment and about sixteen speakers.

'If you're going to do something,' said Pete, 'you might as well do it properly. I mean, Archie, you wouldn't sell a ring-binder with only one ring, would you?'

Dad shook his head.

Jack saw him struggling to think of something to say, like he always did. Jack felt a pang in his tummy, like he always did.

'Hope you've increased your home contents insurance,' said Mum to Uncle Pete. 'You must have spent a packet in here.'

'Only about a hundred and twenty grand,' said Uncle Pete. 'And I don't have to worry about burglars because this baby's got a state-of-the-art security system.'

He picked up the biggest and most expensive-looking remote Jack had ever seen, and pressed one of the buttons. With an expensive-sounding clunk, a metal door slid shut across the doorway they'd come through.

'Impressive,' said Aunty Anthea's new boyfriend Rakesh. 'Controlled by an 87659SLK Quad, I bet. Very fine chip.'

'I told them I wanted the best,' said Uncle Pete.

As he said this, several more clunks, much louder, came from above their heads.

'What was that?' said Aunty Sue, looking alarmed.

Jack saw that Uncle Pete was looking alarmed too. But only for a moment. Then he grinned.

'Must be the soil settling,' he said. 'The builders cracked a pool pipe when they were excavating down here and it started leaking this week, so I got them to dig under the pool and fix it.'

'They were terrified,' said Aunty Sue. 'Pete said he'd have them in the International Court Of Justice if they weren't finished by Friday.'

Uncle Pete rolled his eyes.

'Not the International Court,' he said. 'Just the High Court.'

Jack was about to comment that the sticky tape Dad sold could have fixed the problem, when he noticed water running down the wall behind Uncle Pete. It was trickling in through the ventilation grilles.

'Excuse me, Uncle Pete,' he said, pointing.

But Uncle Pete didn't hear. He was busy talking to the others.

'The walls are packed with clay specially imported from Bolivia,' said Uncle Pete. 'Bolivian clay is brilliant for keeping noise out. Absolutely no sound gets through it.'

'I was able to advise Pete about that,' said Niall. 'My work with the acoustic properties of Bolivian clay in Third World concert halls won me a Guns 'N' Roses Foundation Research Fellowship.'

The others murmured in an impressed way.

'My research methodology was quite simple,'

said Niall. 'I didn't have a shower for three weeks in Bolivia and discovered I couldn't hear my noisy neighbours due to the build-up of clay in my ears.'

The others murmured in an even more impressed way. Then Mum noticed something.

'Pete,' she said. 'Why is the floor wet?'

'It's because of that water running down the wall,' said Jack.

Uncle Pete turned, and his eyes went wide. Water was coming in through the ventilation grilles even faster now.

'Jeez,' said Uncle Pete. 'That shouldn't be happening.'

Other family members murmured in agreement.

'Quick,' said Uncle Pete. 'Turn all this gear off.'

He and Uncle Rob dashed around, switching all the equipment off.

By the time they'd finished, water was gushing in. It was up to Jack's ankles.

'Everybody out,' said Uncle Pete.

He stabbed a button on the remote. The door stayed closed. He pushed several more buttons. The door didn't open. He pounded all the buttons. Nothing.

'That's the one problem with the 87659SLK Quad,' said Rakesh. 'Doesn't work if it gets damp.'

Uncle Pete sloshed over to the door and dried as much of it as he could with his shirt tail. He wiped the remote as well. Then he pressed all the buttons again. And again. And again.

The door still didn't move.

The water was nearly up to their knees.

'Don't panic,' said Mum to Jack. It'll start draining away in a sec.'

'No, it won't,' said Uncle Pete. 'This room is completely sealed. I didn't want any humidity warping my turntable.'

'I'll ring for help,' said Aunty Anthea, fumbling with her phone. 'What's the number for the State Emergency Service?'

'Don't bother,' said Niall. 'Bolivian clay totally blocks phone signals. It's got tiny particles of mica in it. The CIA use it in all their buildings.'

The family members all stared at Uncle Pete.

'I had to use it,' protested Uncle Pete. 'Phone signals can affect blu-ray picture quality.'

'Why's the air in here starting to smell stale?' said Uncle Rob.

Aunty Sue sniffed.

'Shouldn't be,' she said. 'It's air-conditioned.'

'I put in a three-phase industrial-quality air-management system with anti-static pollen filters,' said Uncle Pete.

He waded over to the only ventilation grille that didn't have water gushing out of it, reached up and held his hand in front of it.

'Poop,' he said. 'The water must have shorted the air-con motors.'

Aunty Sue gave a sob.

The water was over their knees.

And Jack's waist. He looked frantically around the room. No windows. No more doors. Not even a fire escape.

'We'll have to dig our way out,' said Uncle Rob. 'I've seen it done. The workers at the hospital in Africa had to do it when they were building the staff squash court and some scaffolding collapsed. Most of them survived.'

'They only had to dig through low density African clay,' said Niall. 'Bolivian clay goes hard as steel when it gets wet.'

'We're trapped,' sobbed Aunty Sue. 'We're all going to suffocate.'

'Calm down, woman,' said Uncle Pete. 'There's enough air in here for hours. We'll drown long before the air runs out.'

Everyone sloshed over to the door and started clawing at it. And kicking it. And trying to smash through it with items of electrical equipment. They kept trying until all Uncle Pete's speakers were floating around them in fragments.

The door didn't budge.

Mum screamed.

Jack knew why. The water was over her waist, and nearly up his chin.

'Jack,' yelled Mum. 'Hang on to something. Pick him up somebody.'

Dad grabbed Jack and lifted him up. Jack hadn't realised Dad was so strong. Though now he thought about it, the stationery shop didn't have a forklift, so Dad must get a lot of exercise carrying all the boxes by hand.

'A chair,' said Aunty Sue. 'Get him a chair.'

The adults splashed around for ages until somebody found a chair under the water. Dad carefully helped Jack stand on it.

The water was only up to Jack's waist now.

But it was up to everyone else's chest.

Then the lights went out.

There was quite a lot of shouting and screaming. After a while, Mum yelled at everyone to be quiet, and after another while, they were. Mostly because, as Jack saw in the faint light from Aunty Anthea's phone, which she was holding over her head, the water was up to their chins.

'There must be another way of getting that door open,' spluttered Uncle Rob. 'A mechanical override.'

'There is,' gasped Uncle Pete. 'But it needs a tiny allen key, and the builders lost it.'

Aunty Sue started crying again.

Then Jack had an idea.

'Dad,' he said. 'Have you got a paperclip?'

Dad frowned as he thought about this.

'Paperclip,' he said. 'Paperclip . . .'

Then his face brightened.

'Yes,' he said. 'One of the new Ezyglide Anti-statics. I brought it home to show Mum.'

He rummaged around under the water, and Jack guessed he was going through his pockets.

'Please,' murmured Aunty Anthea desperately. 'Please find it.'

Dad raised his hand out of the water.

He was holding a paperclip.

'Thank God,' sobbed Aunty Sue, and then gurgled as her mouth filled with water.

Jack watched Dad move slowly towards the door, paperclip held high.

Dad reached the door, took a big breath of air and ducked under the surface of the water.

Jack stood on tiptoe to keep the water away from his mouth and counted the seconds.

Forty.

Fifty.

Sixty and still Dad hadn't come back up.

Jack prayed that correction fluid got spilled a lot in stationery shops. The stuff that gave off pongy fumes. Which meant Dad would have had lots of practice holding his breath.

Seventy.

So he wouldn't drown.

Eighty seconds.

Suddenly there was a clunk and a gurgle and a loud sucking sound, and the door started to slide open.

The water level dropped immediately, and the family members screamed and cheered and spluttered and sobbed.

Then the water level stopped going down.

Jack saw why. Outside the door, the steep concrete

steps going up to the garden were preventing the rest of the water from flowing away.

But it didn't matter. The door was open now and daylight was coming in, and fresh air, and the distant sound above them of an automatic pool cleaner sucking itself dry in an empty pool.

And there was Dad, head and shoulders out of the water, staring at the paperclip in his hand with relief and gratitude.

Dad wasn't the only one doing that.

The whole family was gazing at the paperclip that way. And at Dad. And not just with relief and gratitude. With awe and admiration and respect as well.

Jack grinned, careful to keep his mouth closed because with so much panic somebody was bound to have done a wee in the water.

OK, he said to himself as he swam over to Mum and Dad. I admit it. Big family get-togethers aren't so bad after all.

Big Mistake

*I*t all started with bosoms.

When me and Imelda were babies, Mum used to breastfeed us. I loved those meals. I loved them even more than I love spicy sausage pizza now.

Until Imelda spoiled everything.

Even nine years later I can still remember what happened. Me sucking away happily on Mum's left side as usual. Imelda doing the same on the other side. Until suddenly Imelda stopped sucking and glared at me across Mum's valley.

'Donald's bosom is bigger than mine,' she wailed.

Mum didn't know what Imelda's wail meant, of course. But I understood. And Imelda was completely wrong. No way was the bosom in my mouth bigger than the one in hers.

'No, it's not,' I wailed. 'Hers is bigger.'

I'd never compared Mum's bosoms before, but now that Imelda had introduced the topic I could clearly see that my bosom was actually smaller than Imelda's bosom.

'Not fair,' I wailed. 'Hers is much bigger.'

'Rubbish,' wailed Imelda. 'His is.'

Mum didn't have a clue what we were on about. But she could see we weren't happy, so she burped us and checked our nappies for recent visitors and tickled us under our chins and got us sucking again.

Imelda didn't make any more wild accusations that day. Or that year. But every mealtime as she sucked grumpily and glared at me from her side, I could see what she was thinking.

His is bigger.

I glared back.

I was thinking the opposite.

Hers is bigger.

When you're a twin it's very important that the other twin doesn't get more than you. You probably have to be a twin to understand how important that is. How very, very important.

I knew it wasn't going to end with bosoms.

It didn't.

On our first birthday Dad made us a cake in the shape of Thomas the Tank Engine. Me and Imelda both loved Thomas, so we were very happy.

At first.

All our aunties and uncles and grandparents were there and they helped us blow out the candles. We had one candle each. Exactly the same size. I checked and Imelda did too.

Mum cut the cake and gave us half a Fat Controller each.

Imelda's face went red with distress. She pointed at my plate and said her first word.

'Bigger.'

Mum had cut the Fat Controller so we each had one side of his body, including half his bottom. Imelda was saying that my Fat Controller buttock was bigger than her Fat Controller buttock.

Which was rubbish. Hers was bigger.

I pointed at Imelda's plate and said my first two words.

'Bigger buttock.'

We both burst into tears.

All the grown-ups tried to make our birthday happy again. Mum offered us exactly half a coal truck each instead, then realised that one of the coal truck's eyebrows was bigger than the other. Auntie Pauline explained how most people in real life don't have perfectly matching buttocks, and pointed to Uncle John's as an example. Dad got a bowl of icing and a brush and painted some extra underpants on the Fat Controller's buttocks to try and disguise their size, but me and Imelda saw through that.

Poor Mum and Dad.

Every birthday it was the same.

When we were five, me and Imelda both asked for exactly the same birthday present. A tape measure. Mum and Dad gave us one each.

Identical tape measures.

Or so they thought.

Imelda measured my tape measure with hers, and I measured hers with mine, and soon we were both in tears.

'His is .06 of a millimetre longer,' sobbed Imelda.

'Hers is .0003 of a millimetre thicker,' I wailed. 'And her wrapping paper is wider too.'

When we started school, they put Imelda in one class and me in another. It didn't work.

'His teacher is bigger than mine,' wailed Imelda. 'I measured them.'

'Only round the tummy,' I sobbed. 'Hers is taller and has got much bigger feet.'

Every day it was the same.

'His fish fingers are bigger than mine,' sobbed Imelda one evening.

'Hers are,' I wailed.

'They can't be,' shouted Mum. 'They're made in a factory. With millions of dollars' worth of equipment scientifically designed to make sure every fish finger is exactly the same size. That's why we have fish fingers four times a week.'

Imelda and me thought about this.

'It's the way you cook them,' wailed Imelda. 'You make mine shrink.'

'Mine shrink more,' I sobbed.

Mum grabbed our plates and dumped the fish fingers onto the chopping board.

'Right,' she said. 'Here's what we're going to do. You're each going to cut your fish fingers exactly in half. I suggest you use your tape measures. Then you're each going to choose which halves you want, one piece at a time, taking it in turns, so you both end up with exactly the same number of halves, which each of you will have chosen yourself.'

Mum gave a weary sigh.

'Let's see you find a reason for squabbling then,' she said. 'I should have thought of this years ago.'

Mum handed us a knife each.

Me and Imelda grabbed our tape measures and measured the knives.

'His is bigger than mine,' sobbed Imelda.

'Hers is,' I wailed.

The years passed. Nothing changed. Except Mum and Dad got wearier. Sometimes I felt guilty, but I couldn't stop. I couldn't give in. I couldn't let Imelda get more than me. You can't do that, not when you're a twin.

Whenever I thought about the future, I realised life would always be the same in our family. Until Mum and Dad got old and so weary they died. Then the undertaker would send us their ashes, and Imelda would claim I got a bigger share and I'd say she did.

That was our future.

Until last week, when we went on holiday.

I think it was the motel muesli that was the last straw. ('He's got bigger bran flakes than me.' 'She's got bigger particles of hydrogenated kelp.')

Or maybe the last straw was at the service-station cafe. ('She's got a bigger straw than me.'

'His 275-ml carton of chocolate milk is bigger than my 275-ml carton of chocolate milk.')

Or maybe it was the drive up the coast. ('He spilt more chocolate milk on the car seat than I did.' 'She did a bigger sick in the glove box than I did.')

Whichever it was, at lunchtime everything changed.

We were having a picnic in a carpark near the highway. Sandwiches ('hers is crustier') and bananas ('his is more bent').

'For the love of Pete,' said Dad wearily. 'When are you two going to grow up and stop whingeing and complaining?'

I looked around at the other families having picnics. Happy laughing families with kids who weren't squabbling and parents who weren't weary and miserable.

I looked at their cars. None of them had luggage on the roof like ours. Probably because they didn't have an extra bag full of tape measures and rulers and microscopes and weighing scales and surveyor's tripods and portable laser measuring devices.

Suddenly I felt weary and miserable too.

I wanted our family to be one of the happy ones.

We'd eaten most of our picnic. There were just two bananas left. You didn't need a measuring device to see that one was big and one was small.

Mum and Dad were pretending those bananas didn't exist. I could see they were hoping me and Imelda would do the same.

I picked up the big one and held it out to Imelda. 'Here,' I said. 'You have it.'

Imelda stared at me, stunned.

So did Mum and Dad.

'You want me to have the big banana?' said Imelda, amazed.

I nodded. I could see Imelda's mind working fast. Her eyes narrowed. I could see she was looking for the catch.

Then she grinned.

'No thanks,' she said. 'I don't need it.'

I was confused. Was she saying she wanted me to have it?

Before I could decide, Imelda jumped up, grabbed hold of my hand and dragged me round the other side of a big parked truck.

'I don't need your banana,' she said sweetly. 'I've got a bigger banana than you'll ever have.'

I stared.

In front of us was a gigantic banana. It must have been at least 30 metres long. And three times as tall as a grown-up. It looked like it was made of plastic. On the side of it was a sign.

The Big Banana, Coffs Harbour, NSW.

'I win,' said Imelda.

For a moment I hoped this was just a silly game. That we were having fun like the other families. But Imelda was looking at me in a very mocking way and I could see from her eyes that she was deadly serious.

I realised what had happened.

Imelda had listened to Dad and decided he was right. We were too old for whingeing and complaining. Now we were ten, she'd decided, we were old enough for gloating and winning.

Everything had changed, and nothing had.

She'd won with the banana. I knew there couldn't be a bigger banana anywhere in Australia. But that was only Round One.

Later that afternoon, further up the highway, we passed The Big Prawn and I spotted it first, which made it mine.

'I've got a bigger prawn than you,' I gloated.

Imelda seethed.

In the front of the car, Mum and Dad, who'd been feeling a bit light-headed from three whole hours without any whingeing and complaining, sagged into their seats.

The rest of the week was a nightmare.

As we toured around on our driving holiday, me and Imelda couldn't relax for a second. We hardly dared blink in case we missed something.

I got The Big Peanut, The Big Crab and I was in the middle of gloating to Imelda that I had a bigger bottom than her when Mum wearily pointed out that what I'd just seen wasn't The Big Buttock, it was a haystack covered with pink plastic.

Imelda got The Big Pineapple, The Big Cow and what she claimed was The Big Swimming Pool, which it wasn't because it was a lake.

'Cheat,' I sneered at her.

'Jealous,' she sneered back.

'Please,' sighed Mum wearily.

We'd never been more unhappy.

I started imagining big things and desperately hoping they'd be round the next corner so I could see them first and win.

The Big Flyscreen.

The Big Teabag.

The Big Blood Clot if we passed an abattoir.

Nothing.

Dad started going out of his way to avoid big things. He saw in a tourist brochure that the next town had The Big Tow Truck, so he took a dirt track through a swamp to keep us away from it.

We got bogged in the mud.

While Mum and Dad tried to get us out, me and Imelda gathered dry grass and branches to put under the back wheels. Except Imelda wasn't doing much gathering. She was too busy gloating.

'I've got bigger bosoms than you,' she said in a very cocky voice.

I looked up.

Imelda was sneering at me and pointing towards the horizon. In the distance, next to what must have been the highway, was a huge advertising billboard with an ad for a caravan park. Most of it was a woman with half her bosoms showing.

I stared at it for a long time.

Imelda kept on gloating for a long time.

I didn't care. I was thinking about a long time ago, when all this had started. When Imelda reckoned I had the biggest bosom and I reckoned she did.

We couldn't both have been right. Then another thought hit me. What if we'd both been wrong? What if Mum's bosoms were exactly the same size? All this whingeing and complaining and gloating and winning wouldn't be necessary anymore.

Suddenly I wanted to know the truth.

That night, in the motel, I took a peek.

Mum was having a shower. Dad and Imelda were watching a movie on TV. During an exciting bit when they were totally engrossed, I crept over to the bathroom, opened the door and peeped in.

Just as I did, the shower screen slid open and Mum stepped out.

She saw me looking.

'Oh, for Pete's sake,' she said, grabbing a towel and wrapping it around herself. 'Can't a person get a moment's peace in this family?'

My guts went tight and cold. Not because Mum was annoyed. Because of what I'd seen.

Mum's left bosom was slightly bigger than her right one. And it hung slightly lower. Which made it seem even larger.

'What's wrong, love?' said Mum.

She must have noticed my miserable face.

'Imelda was right,' I said sadly.

'Right about what?' said Mum.

'That my bosom was bigger than hers,' I said.

'Of course I was right,' said Imelda, coming over. She gave me a jealous look. 'Your bosom was always bigger.'

Mum frowned and looked puzzled.

Then she grinned.

'What a pair of nongs,' she said.

For a moment I thought she was talking about her bosoms. But then I saw she wasn't, she was talking about me and Imelda.

'You didn't have a bosom each,' said Mum. 'You couldn't. The right-hand one didn't feed properly. The milk kept getting blocked. So I fed you both with the left one, taking turns.'

I stared at her.

'But I can remember us both sucking at once,' I said. 'I can remember it.'

'So can I,' said Imelda.

Mum shook her head.

'Nope,' she said.

'Wasn't possible,' said Dad, joining us.

'When we get home,' said Mum, 'I'll show you the doctor's report from the baby health centre. I was a lefty. That's why it sags a bit now.'

I looked at Imelda. I could see she was as shocked as I was.

'The right one was a waiting and burping area,' said Mum. 'While one of you was feeding on the left side, I'd cuddle the other one of you on the right side.'

Me and Imelda stood there for a long time, just staring at Mum's towel-covered chest.

Mum let us. I think she could see that me and Imelda had some important things to think about.

'Don't you mind?' I said to Mum after a while. 'That we made one of them a bit saggy?'

'Course not,' said Mum. 'It's what it's for. Anyway, when I've got a pair of anything, I always like them both exactly the same amount.'

Dad nodded.

Mum gave me and Imelda a long look.

I realised she wasn't just talking about her bosoms.

I glanced over and saw that Imelda had realised this too. She opened her mouth to say something. I wondered if she was going to boast about having a worse memory than me.

For a moment I wanted to be the one to boast about having the worst memory.

But I didn't.

I decided to give Imelda the chance.

Imelda stayed silent.

After a while I realised she was giving me the chance.

We stood there, glancing at each other nervously. Then we swapped a little grin. Mum gave us both a hug. And at last there was no need for me or Imelda to say anything.

Harriet's Story

Harriet wakes up.

She can't see anything except the dull glow of her bedside clock.

3.14 a.m.

That explains why the rest of her bedroom is dark. Darker than the inside of a black sock that's been swallowed by a large bat who lives in a cave with very thick curtains.

Strange, thinks Harriet. I don't usually wake up in the middle of the night. And if I do, I don't usually lie here making up weird sentences about how dark it is.

She wonders what's going on.

Then she realises.

She's thirsty. Very thirsty. Thirstier than a blast-furnace operator lost in the middle of the Sahara desert who forgot to have a drink before he went on holiday.

Of course, thinks Harriet. That's why I've woken up. And that's why I'm making up these weird sentences. My brain's dehydrated.

Easily fixed.

Harriet switches on her lamp and reaches for the glass of water Mum always leaves on the bedside table.

The glass is empty. Emptier than a cave whose usual inhabitant, a large hungry sock-eating bat, has rushed off to the Sahara after hearing that an overheated blast-furnace operator has just taken off his shoes.

Harriet blinks.

This thirst, she thinks, is really making me think weird things.

Oh well, still easily fixed.

Plenty to drink in the kitchen. Water in the tap. Juice in the fridge. Long-life milk in the cupboard if I feel like a long life.

Harriet gets out of bed, opens her bedroom door and creeps out. She closes the door quietly behind her.

The hallway isn't as dark as her room. There's a faint haze of moonlight coming through a window.

This is more sort of gloomy than dark, thinks Harriet. As gloomy as a bat in the desert staring at two socks it can't eat because it's allergic to polyester.

Stop it, Harriet says to herself.

The kitchen.

She doesn't turn the hallway light on. Mustn't wake Mum and Dad. They both work hard and need their sleep.

As Harriet creeps past their room, she hears gentle snoring. And wheezing. And slobbering.

Muttley must be sleeping on their bed.

Just the thought of her beloved dog makes Harriet's insides go warm. Almost as warm as the polyester-sock soup a hungry bat might make to try and get some of the sock flavour without having to swallow any of the actual . . .

Harriet concentrates on getting down the stairs to the kitchen.

Luckily there are some glints of moonlight on the stairs. She goes down carefully, step by step, counting each stair silently to keep her mind from wandering.

. . . three, four, five . . .

She stops.

Gleaming on the next stair is a small plastic racing car.

Typical, she thinks. Younger brothers always leave their toys where other people could step on them and do triple backward somersaults down the stairs and land on their pelvises and sprain their anterior fibulate cartilages and miss out on selection for the school swimming team.

Harriet reminds herself that Billy is only four and probably didn't mean it.

Then the moonlight disappears.

The plastic racing car glows eerily. Particularly around the headlights.

Strange.

Harriet didn't think racing cars had headlights.

She stands in the darkness, feeling a bit spooked. She's read about this. Hallucinations. Seeing things. It can happen to people who are extremely thirsty. She read a story only recently about somebody dying of thirst in a desert who thought a large bat was eating his socks.

Mum. Dad. Help.

Harriet wants to call out. She wants Mum and Dad to wake up and switch on the light and stumble concerned out of their room and trip over Muttley and do triple backward somersaults down the stairs and land on their pelvises and sprain their anterior fibulate cartilages and miss out on . . .

No, she doesn't.

It's OK, Harriet tells herself. I'm not in the desert. I'm standing on the stairs at home. People don't usually die of thirst standing on the stairs, even when they feel like they might.

Slowly, carefully, she moves down the dark steps towards the kitchen.

. . . eleven, twelve, thirteen . . .

She knows there are fifteen steps because that's how Mum and Dad taught her to count, years ago. But she prepares herself for a few more now, maybe a few hundred more, because that's what happens when you're hallucinating from thirst.

. . . fourteen, fifteen . . .

She tests ahead with her foot.

No more.

Just flat floor.

Good, the hallucinations have stopped.

Harriet walks towards the kitchen, very slowly and carefully because this downstairs hall is darker than a . . .

Stop that.

She can't see the kitchen door, but she knows roughly how far it is from the bottom of the stairs. She holds her hands up in front of her in case the hallucinations start again and she bumps into a stuffed gorilla or a big pile of bat poo or the Eiffel Tower.

Bump.

Her fingers are touching something. It doesn't feel lumpy or pooey or French.

It feels like a door handle.

Yes.

The kitchen door.

At last she can get a drink.

Harriet turns the handle, steps into the kitchen and quietly closes the door. Now she can switch the light on without disturbing Mum and Dad.

She does.

At first the brightness hurts her eyes. She can't see anything. All she can think of is thirst. She wants to rush to the fridge and grab the bottle of juice and glug it down, blind and squinting. But she doesn't.

There are other bottles and jars in the fridge she wouldn't want to grab by mistake. Soy sauce. Dad's home-made ginger beer.

Instead Harriet turns away from the glare and waits for her eyes to adjust. Which they do. Soon she can see the back of the kitchen door clearly.

She can also see a big shadow looming over her.

Somebody else is in the kitchen.

Somebody big.

From the shape of the shadow, it doesn't look like Mum or Dad or Billy. It looks like a man with the sort of very broad shoulders a burglar would probably have. And over one of his shadow shoulders is what looks like a huge sack. Bulging with something very big inside it.

Probably the fridge, thinks Harriet.

She wants to run.

She wants to claw open the kitchen door and leap up the stairs and fling herself into bed with Mum and Dad.

But her hands are sweaty with fear and she knows that if she tries to grab the door handle her fingers will probably slip and she'll be fumbling and the burglar will have heaps of time to grab her and put her in his sack.

She has to think of something else.

Behind her, the burglar isn't saying anything.

He's probably in shock too, thinks Harriet. Burglars are probably cowards underneath, which is why they slink around stealing fridges in the dark.

Harriet has an idea. She decides to turn and face the burglar and pretend she's braver than she is. She'll offer him a deal. If she can have the juice, he can take the fridge.

She turns, guts twisted tighter than a polyester sock. And blinks.

There isn't a burglar.

Just Mum's ski suit, hanging from the light fitting. The hood has flopped over to one side and is making a big sack-shaped shadow.

Harriet remembers Mum saying the ski suit has to go to the drycleaners. She must have hung it here so she wouldn't forget.

Dizzy with relief, and thirst, Harriet pulls the fridge door open, almost tasting the cool sweet juice.

She grabs the juice bottle.

It's empty.

So's the milk.

Dad's ginger beer fermentation jar is lying broken in the bottom of the fridge. Most of the ginger beer has leaked out and been soaked up by the leftover curry and rice in the salad crisper.

Harriet stares, horrified.

There's only one person who'd drink everything in the fridge that carelessly.

Harriet knows she should be waking Mum and Dad and telling them the bad news so they can inform the insurance company and get some more ginger beer yeast for Dad and call the police to see if there's a Younger Brother Punishment Squad.

But first she absolutely must have a drink.

Harriet grabs a glass from the cupboard and goes to the sink and turns the tap on.

Nothing comes out.

She turns the tap on more. Still nothing. She tries the hot tap. Nothing.

The taps are completely dry. Drier than a pair of socks that have been lying in the desert sun so long you wouldn't even know a bat had tried to make soup out of them.

Oh no, thinks Harriet. I'm making up weird sentences again.

Another thought hits her.

Is it just a coincidence the fridge is empty and the water pipes are dry on the same night? Or is something else going on?

Like . . .

Like . . .

Harriet can't imagine what it could be. She thinks about the moonlight disappearing, and the plastic racing car going spooky, and the burglar-shaped shadow. And now suddenly here's a drought or a burst water main or a clogged valve at the reservoir. Everything that's happened since she got out of bed has made it harder for her to get a drink.

Getting a drink should be so simple.

Not a big problem.

Unless . . .

Suddenly Harriet has to sit down on a kitchen chair.

Could it be . . .?

Last week in class Ms Lovett was talking about stories and how they work. How in every story, the main character must have a problem. And how the character never solves the problem straight away, because that would make the story too short and too boring.

'In a story,' Ms Lovett said, 'things always come along to make the problem harder to solve. Things always get worse before they get better.'

Harriet thinks again about the empty glass and the racing car and the dark hall and scary shadow and the empty juice bottle and the dry taps.

Could it be, she thinks, that I'm in a story?

No, that's crazy.

Harriet goes to the cupboard, finds the long-life milk, and opens the carton. She tips the milk into the glass. Except she doesn't because nothing comes out. She shakes the carton. The contents feel solid. And now there's a cheesy smell.

She looks more closely at the carton to make sure Mum didn't buy long-life cheese by mistake. No, it says long-life milk. Right next to where it says *Use By September 2009*.

Harriet puts the carton down.

She's tempted to ring Ms Lovett for advice. But it's 3.25 a.m, and she knows teachers don't get paid overtime.

No, thinks Harriet, I'll deal with this myself.

She remembers something else Ms Lovett said.

As characters battle to solve their problems, they often discover they're braver than they ever thought they were.

Harriet isn't feeling particularly brave at the moment, but definitely more determined.

And thirstier.

My problem, she says to herself, is getting a drink. If I'm in a story, things will keep coming along to make it harder for me to solve my problem.

Let's put it to the test.

Harriet thinks about what she can do next.

Of course. If a person finds themself in a drinkless kitchen, there's an obvious solution. Go out into the garden and drink from the fish pond.

Harriet opens the kitchen window and peers out. The moon is glowing again and the pond is rippling, but the trees around it are full of bats. They're fruit bats and Harriet knows they're harmless, but she also knows it's best not to drink anything that's directly under a bat's bottom.

She closes the window.

OK, she thinks. I need another way to fix the problem. How about waking up Mum and Dad and asking them to drive me to the all-night supermarket? It's only a ten-minute journey.

Harriet takes a couple of steps towards the stairs, then stops.

She's thinking of all the things that could happen on the way to the supermarket to stop her solving her problem.

Dad crashing the car into the library.

The whole family being abducted by aliens and taken to a planet where the inhabitants live on a diet of really salty crisps and curried sand.

Mum being pulled over for not wearing a seatbelt and then being charged with the desert murder of a sockless blast-furnace operator.

Mind you, there would probably be a water cooler at the police station . . .

No.

Harriet sits down again and thinks hard. She needs a way of solving her problem that won't put Mum and Dad in danger and cause them to lose sleep and/or their car and/or their freedom and/or their library tickets.

Of course, she says to herself. Why didn't I think of it before? I'll break into our neighbours' house and borrow a drink from them.

Harriet creeps out the back door, staying well away from the fruit bats, climbs over the fence and runs, crouching, across the neighbours' lawn.

At their house, trying to feel braver than she ever has before, she looks for a possible place to break in.

And finds one. An open toilet window. It's a bit high up, but if she stands on this garden table, and pulls herself up using this metal box screwed to the wall with the little red flickering light on it . . .

Oops, thinks Harriet as she jumps back down from the table. That burglar alarm wasn't there last time I looked.

Yet another thing making her problem harder to solve.

As Harriet hurries away from the neighbours' house, she remembers something else Ms Lovett said about stories. How trying to solve a problem can sometimes cause an even bigger problem.

She also remembers something Dad said about the neighbours. How they collect Olympic swimming medals, buying them from all over the world, and how they're always worrying that their priceless collection will be burgled.

That would have been a bigger problem alright, thinks Harriet. If the neighbours had caught me in their house and thought I was trying to steal their medals, and had rung the police. The Older Sister Crime Squad would have been round in a flash.

As Harriet crosses the lawn, she notices that a trench has recently been dug and filled in again. A trench from the street to the neighbours' house.

A cable's probably been laid, she thinks. A high-security burglar alarm cable that has to go under the ground.

Wait a minute.

When a deep high-security trench is dug, perhaps it can sometimes damage other things under the ground. Like water pipes.

Harriet hurries out to the street, to where the trench meets the footpath. She peers at the ground. And sees exactly what she was hoping to see.

A big patch of damp mud.

She's so thirsty now she's tempted just to fill her mouth with mud and see if she can suck any water out of it.

But she doesn't. She hurries to the shed, finds Dad's pickaxe, comes back and digs down into the mud.

Yes.

There it is.

Just as she'd suspected.

She's uncovered the place where the water pipe to her house joins the main pipe for the street. In the house pipe, near the join, is a crack with water trickling out of it.

Harriet drops to her knees and laps at the water. It's muddy and gritty, but she doesn't care.

All she cares about is there's not enough of it.

The tantalising taste of water is driving her crazy with thirst.

She grabs the pickaxe and swings it gently and makes the crack in the pipe just a little bit bigger. Mud and plastic putty ooze out of the crack.

Look at that, thinks Harriet. When they dug the trench, they not only cracked our pipe, they tried to hide what they'd done with plastic putty.

She swings the pickaxe again and makes the crack a little bit bigger again.

Well, quite a bit bigger actually, but Harriet doesn't care because now the water is bubbling out in a glorious fountain and she plunges her face into it and drinks and drinks and drinks.

And drinks.

Ahhhh, that's better.

Problem solved.

Suddenly Harriet is dizzy with tiredness. She has just enough strength to block the hole in the pipe with the putty and her socks, put the pickaxe back in the shed, and drag herself up to bed.

She flops down and closes her eyes, and as the warm tide of sleep carries her away, she has one last thought.

That's nice, she murmurs to herself. My story has a happy ending.

So deep is Harriet's sleep she doesn't hear the faint pop of a plug of putty and sock being expelled from a hole in a water pipe, and the soft gush of water fountaining high into the night sky and then cascading down a driveway and under the neighbours' front door.

Hours later she's still slumbering so soundly that even the harsh sound of a State Emergency Service diesel pump starting up on the other side of the fence doesn't wake her. Nor does the even harsher sound of the neighbours wailing about possible rust damage to their medals.

Somebody the noise does wake, though, in the next street, is Ms Lovett.

Hmmm, thinks Ms Lovett, stretching sleepily under the covers with the contentment of a person who loves her job. I think I'll talk to the class some more about stories today. Introduce them to irony.

Perhaps use the example of a character solving a problem and causing another problem that's the exact opposite.

She pauses, reflecting.

Are they ready for irony, this lot?

She stretches again, smiling.

Yes, I think so.

ALSO BY MORRIS GLEITZMAN

Doubting Thomas

The truth is . . .
Thomas has an embarrassing secret.
Is it a rare and special gift or the worst thing
that could happen to a boy?

A story about best friends, surprising
adventures and itchy nipples.

Grace

In the beginning there was me and Mum and Dad
and the twins. And talk about happy families, we were
bountiful. But it came to pass that I started doing sins.
And lo, that's when all our problems began.

Bumface

His mum calls him Mr Dependable,
but Angus can barely cope. Another baby would
be a disaster. So Angus comes up with a bold and
brave plan to stop her getting pregnant.
That's when he meets Rindi.
And Angus thought *he* had problems . . .

AVAILABLE FROM PUFFIN

About the Author

Morris Gleitzman grew up in England and came to Australia when he was sixteen. He was a frozen-chicken thawer, sugar-mill rolling-stock unhooker, fashion-industry trainee, student, department-store Santa, TV producer, newspaper columnist and screenwriter. Then twenty-five years ago he had a wonderful experience. He wrote a novel for young people. Since then he's been one of Australia's most popular children's authors.

Visit Morris at his website:
morrisgleitzman.com